Soulmate

EUFRAGIO MANGUELE

BlueRose ONE.com
Stories Matter

BLUEROSE PUBLISHERS UK Ltd.
London

This book is primarily published and distributed in Great Britain and is also available in other global marketplaces.

BlueRose ONE.com
Stories Matter

ISBN: 978-93-6783-720-7

Designed and distributed by **BlueRoseONE.com** with global reach. Printing and fulfilment are managed through international distribution networks, ensuring availability based on order locations.

For publishing inquiries, visit **www.BlueRoseONE.com**

BlueRose Publishers UK Ltd,
Unit 3, 6-7 St Mary at Hill, London

+44 7386286323

First Edition: April 2025

Acknowledgements And Dedication

To God, our Father and Creator, who has demonstrated unconditional love for us on numerous occasions throughout my life.

To my father, Amândio Carlos Manguele, who departed us in 2018 to be with our creator. My father has always encouraged me to strive for the best and taught me never to be a conformist. His encouragement and guidance have continued to aid me on my journey. I will always be grateful for everything he taught me.

To my mother, Gracinda André Muzime, who has dedicated her entire life to her family. You are my Angel and the brightness of my life.

To my other half, Zuzana Staffova, who has been by my side every day, through highs and lows. Thank you for your hard work and unwavering love. You are my soulmate.

To Nick and Ankita of BlueRose Publishers. Thank you, Nick, for insisting on me and forcing me to never give up and pursue this dream. Ankita, I appreciate all of your attention and for making me feel like a true writer with a supporting team for the first time in my life.

This book, despite being a work of fiction, seeks to remind us of the most vital aspects of life. Our mindless pursuit of happiness through materialism has instilled in us the mentality of selfishness and self-destruction. The spread of the self-love mindset has led to a society in which no one sees other's feelings and thoughts, and we are gradually destroying ourselves as individuals and society. I hope that while reading this book, you will not only find it to be a beautiful and intriguing love tale, but also develop, or rediscover, the true principles that can help us all construct a better society.

Eufragio Manguele

Contents

Chapter 1

Goodbye Portsmouth

It was a drizzling day, Gabriel was sitting inside the bus, observing the drops of rain, which resembled tears flowing down on the large window of the bus. He had just finished the job and was going home. It was his last day on his job as a waiter. For 12 months he worked in a PUB in the city of Portsmouth. Despite the fact that he had to constantly coexist with the noisy and preposterous beer-consuming customers who were always ready to complain about the most insignificant thing, like for instance, a delay of their beverage or the absence of a waiter to take their order seconds after they sat down, he enjoyed working there. He had met some interesting people who had taught him good things. So, on his last day, his soul was filled with excitement and sadness at the same time. He was excited and happy because of the new adventure ahead of him but was sad because he was leaving behind people who helped him and had been part of his life for the past 12 months.

On the bus, he reflected on all that had happened for the past year. It was thought-provoking that, about a month ago, he was so excited and praying for the time to pass quickly, but now that the time had passed and he was about to start the new adventure, his excitement was mixed with sadness. He tried to find out the reason his soul wasn't thrilled with happiness and, at that moment, he realised how important his job and colleagues had been to him. The last day at work had been special. His colleagues had prepared a goodbye party for him. He received many gifts and cards with emotive words. They even made a cake for him and opened a bottle of sparkling wine to celebrate with him and wish him good luck on his new adventure. A certain lady, who during the past 12 months had the same shifts as him and, therefore, was one of his closest colleagues had given him a very special gift. She gave him a white Orchid, with splendour flowers that would embellish the environment wherever they would be placed. He had the plant with him, on his lap, holding it with much care, the one which any delicate and precious item would require.

While lost in his thoughts, the bus came to a bus stop, in front of a local hospital, and there, he saw a man. It seemed to him that the man was crying. It was hard to see because of the rain, and Gabriel wasn't sure if what he had seen were tears or drops of rain falling on the face of the man. Gabriel then thought to himself - "*What would make a man of that age cry, and principally, in a public place?*". - The answers to that question were infinite, anything could be possible. He could be crying because of love, because of work, because of health, or, maybe, because of the weather. Gabriel then smiled and, in his mind, said to himself - "*I hope he is crying because of the weather, it's less painful than any other thing*".

The city of Portsmouth is located on the south coast of England. It is considered one of the warmest places in the country and the whole of Britain. However, just like the whole British island, as soon as autumn arrived, at the beginning of October, the cold breeze, accompanied by showers, characterised the city's weather. On that particular day, it was raining the whole time.

Gabriel couldn't stop thinking about the man that was crying. He had somehow, sympathized with the man, wishing he could have helped him. He reflected on how hard it is to see a person crying and not feel bad about it. It is like a reminder that sadness is still around, even when we are in our happiest moment, someone, nearby or far away, is experiencing sadness. It is as if the entity responsible for happiness and sadness needs to balance it, to keep the world functioning. Gabriel was going to start a new journey, in a new place, and was happy about it. For the past month, he had forgotten what is to be sad, but as he saw that man, he remembered that sadness is always in the corner, trying to steal the smile from our faces.

He imagined if the man had his children in hospital, and thought about how hard it is for the parents to see their children infirm. Would any parent be able to concentrate on anything else? Probably not. Gabriel then asked himself, - "*Why am I thinking about something so terrible?*" - He decided to forget the man and concentrate on what was ahead. Strangely, he felt guilty for deciding to stop figuring out what had happened with the man, he felt somehow selfish, but he didn't want to go back to those thoughts. He placed the Orchid on the empty seat next to him and opened his bag to grab a book to read. The book was about Myths and Legends of the world. His girlfriend had given the book to him and for more than 6 months the book was his companion on his journeys to and from work. Her name was Alena and they have been living together for about one and a half years. They had been taking care of each other almost since the day they met.

One and a half years before, Gabriel had moved to live close to her. Before that, they had been friends, good friends. They were living in different countries when they noticed that their feelings surpassed friendship, and they decided they had to be together, in the same place.

Alena was at university and couldn't move to live next to him, therefore, it was Gabriel who moved to Portsmouth and since then their life has been of a family of 2, caring, making plans, loving, advising, and being happy. They were an incredible couple and knew each other very well.

In Portsmouth, Gabriel found work as a waiter in a local PUB. He graduated in Hotel Management and has worked in many areas of the hotel industry. However, when he arrived in Portsmouth, the whole world was facing a crisis and the tourism industry was the most affected one. It took time until he found a job and for about 5 months they lived on his savings plus the money that Alena was earning as a housekeeper in a hotel where she worked part-time.

When he found a job, things changed for them. They started saving money every month. They saved money for their future project, which was a nature-based accommodation centre. They dreamed about having a bed and breakfast facility in the middle of nature. They were nature lovers and wanted to do something that, while would pay their bills, would also allow them to protect nature.

What they were earning wasn't that much, but they were organized and managed to save something every month. They had another plan, a shorter time plan. They decided that after Alena finished her studies, they would move to the USA, where they would work for 3 or 5 years, and then go back home to start their project.

Alena had just finished her studies and they had succeeded in finding a job in the USA. That is why Gabriel had his last day at his job as a waiter in Portsmouth. By the end of the month, he and Alena were going to the USA, to start a new Journey.

After one hour of the journey by bus, Gabriel arrived home. Alena, as always, was there, waiting for him, smiling, and receiving him with love. He never told her, but that was his best moment of the day. To arrive home and be welcomed by her. Looking at her smile, was like being born over and over again, and each time, discovering new and magnificent things.

- How are you?- Alena asked, while taking his bag from the floor, where he had left it, and placed it in the right place.

Gabriel wasn't a disorganized person but every day, when he came home from work, he left his bag on the floor. Alena was always calling his attention to that, but she ended up just picking it up for him. His work was hard and needed him to use both physical and mental effort. He loved customer service, but sometimes it could be hard and stressful. So when he arrived home he just wanted to ease it down.

- I am good. Thank you. And how was your day?
- It was good too. I talked with my mom.
- Good, how is she?
- She is good. She said hello to you. She can't wait to see us.

Alena had finished her studies in July, but they stayed in Portsmouth until October because it was when they would go to the USA. After finishing her studies, Alena continued with her work as a housekeeper until the end of September. Now that Gabriel had finished his work, they would travel to the Czech Republic, the homeland of Alena, where they would stay for 3 weeks before travelling to the USA.

- How was the last day of the work? – Alena asked Gabriel.
- It was good. My colleagues had a surprise prepared for me. They even brought a cake, it's a pity that I couldn't eat it. I felt bad.

Gabriel was allergic to dairy and gluten, his colleagues forgot about it when they made his cake. He didn't eat the cake at work but he brought one piece of it to Alena.

- I brought a piece of it for you.
- Thank you. It's chocolate!!! I like it.
- Everyone likes chocolate, I don't understand why.
- You are just jealous that you can't eat it.
- You think?
- I am sure. But don't worry, I made something that you love for dinner.
- Thank you. I can't wait to eat. Let me take a shower.

While Gabriel was in the shower, Alena prepared dinner. She had already eaten and, therefore, she placed it just for him. It was like that every time that Gabriel worked evening shifts. He would come home from work, and he would eat while Alena was there, sitting by his side.

After he finished his shower, he went to sit down. Alena had already the food on the table and while sitting, waiting for him. She said:

- It is incredible, isn't it?
- What is it?
- We are leaving. In two days we will say goodbye to Portsmouth.
- Yes, it is.
- I have been living here for 3 years. I will never forget this place. I will miss our apartment as well, our very first apartment together.

Alena and Gabriel lived in a rented one-bedroom apartment. It was small but cosy. The kitchen and the living room were connected, just separated by a bar. All the walls of the apartment were painted white and they had decorated them with paintings and pictures. In the living room, they had one small table with 4 chairs, one couch, and one small library station. Over the library, they had a lamp and a projector that they used to watch films. The projector was a Christmas gift from Gabriel to Alena. They had also 5 pots with flowers placed around the living room and in the kitchen, there were pots with pepper plants, small avocado trees, and tomato plants. On the right of the library station, there was a window that had a view of the yard of the building.

Gabriel looked over the apartment and said:

- That is true, I will miss it too. We created good memories here.
- Yes, we grew up as adults and as a couple here. We learned a lot of things.
- Yes, we did. It will be a special place for us, it is a big part of our story together.

They looked at each other with a smile and Alena, who was sitting in front of Gabriel, moved forward and kissed him. He then asked:

- What else will you miss in this city?
- I don't really know. You know that I don't like the city. I like our apartment, but the city itself, not that much. But, there are things that we do that I will miss.

- Which things?
- I will miss our walks by the seaside, or in the rose garden. I will miss our walks in the parks as well. You chasing the squirrels, like a little child. – They both laughed, and Gabriel said:
- I don't chase them, I play with them. You just don't understand.
- I understand, you play with squirrels.
- You should try it, it's funny, and they like it.

Gabriel and Alena liked animals, but Gabriel liked to play with them. Whenever they were in the parks, he would chase the squirrels and when they were on the beach he would chase the seagulls.

- Yes, I will definitely miss that. -Alena said that, while she was smiling. Then she asked Gabriel:
- And you? What will you miss?
- I will miss the same things as you. But what I will miss the most is the sunset, I will miss the days that we go to the big tree in the park, we climb it and watch the sunset.
- I will miss that too.

They had a favourite place to see the sunset. It was a tree in the middle of the park, close to the sea. They would go to the tree, climb it, and watch the sunset. It was a beautiful image, but they decided to not take a picture of it. They had this promise that every time they saw something incredible, they would just admire it, and register it only in their memories and hearts.

- Do you remember the day when a man came to the tree and asked us if we had seen his phone? We said we hadn't, but he didn't believe us.
- Of course, I do. It was funny. I mean, funny for us, but, unfortunately, sad for him.

One day, when they were watching their sunset, a couple approached them and asked if they hadn't seen a mobile phone. They hadn't seen it and told that to the man. The man didn't believe them and made indirect threats to them. In the beginning, they decided to ignore but as the man continued speaking, they decided to leave the place.

- Do you think that he found his phone? – Alena asked.
- I hope so, so he will learn not to accuse people.
- This place will really give us many stories to tell.
- Sure it will. The food was amazing, sunshine, thank you.
- I am happy that you liked it.
- It is impossible not to enjoy your food.
- That is good, it means that you will never eat somewhere else.

They both laughed while looking at each other.

- What about the university? You made friends there. – Gabriel asked Alena.
- Sure I will miss it, but I have to say, it was a little disappointing. Don't get me wrong, it was good to go to university and I did learn interesting things, but overall it seems to me as if it wasn't necessary to go there to learn what I know.

- Why do you say that?
- Well, I didn't like the fact that we, as students, are not allowed to create our own theories or bring our views to the studying field. Everything that I wrote in an essay had to be referenced.
- I understand! Do you think that there was no space for creativity?
- Yes. I know that one part of the academic curriculum is investigation. We must know how to investigate and use already proven facts before making any statement. That's good and comprehensive. However, I think that the investigation field should be open to new theories that might or might not, be based on something that had been written before.
- Hmm, I guess it is complicated when you feel that all you do is copy-paste, I believe that some students may lose interest in the subjects.
- That's what happened to me.
- But you did your best, I think that you were an incredible student and focused.
- I had to be. I couldn't play around. The university is very expensive. But it's all done now. It is late, let's go to bed, I am tired.

Gabriel stood up and went to wash his plate. After that, they went to brush their teeth. When Alena was preparing for sleep, Gabriel played a song and invited her to dance. It was the song "Wonderful Tonight" by Eric Clapton. It was Gabriel's tradition to dance with Alena before sleeping. He didn't do it every day, but at least 3 or 4 times a week. He chose the songs according to his feelings at the moment. That night, he felt wonderful, and it was thanks to Alena that he felt that way. She was wonderful to him.

Chapter 2

The Engine of the world

The following day was going to be their last at Portsmouth, and in England. The city and country where they had been living for the past years. Gabriel woke up earlier than usual. He used to wake up early to prepare for work, but on his day-off, he used to wake up a bit later, to rest his body from many hours of work. That day, although he didn't have work, he still woke up earlier. He couldn't sleep, he was anxious. He spent most of the night just thinking about the new adventure, about how exciting their lives would be. He couldn't hold his anxiety so he decided that the best would be to get up and start doing something that would keep him calm and help to speed the hands of time. Before getting up, he took his mobile phone and looked at the time, it was eight minutes past six. He wondered what he could do at that time. He didn't want to disturb Alena. He sat on the bed and looked at her "*She sleeps like an Angel*" he thought to himself. Right after, while still staring at her he questioned his thoughts: "*Do angels sleep?*" and answered, "*I hope they don't because they have to keep the demons away from us*". The way he was questioning himself and answering his own questions, was as if he was in a room with more than two people having a debate about angels and their role in our world. He didn't realise, but ten minutes had passed while he was staring at her, and his hand was touching, smoothly, her hair. He didn't know when he started to touch her hair, it had been an automatic gesture of his body to touch her while his mind was admiring her. He then decided to stand up and go running. It would be the last time that he would run by the seaside of Portsmouth. Silently he dressed up and then went to the bathroom to wash his face and brush his teeth. Before going to run, he ate an apple, drank some water and kissed Alena on her head.

Gabriel's run lasted about an hour, his favourite part was when he was by the seaside but before arriving there, he had to pass through a few commercial streets. Passing in front of shops, and trying to dodge people walking on sideways who, most of the time, wouldn't pay attention to what was happening and, if he wasn't careful, he would easily crush with them. When he arrived at the seaside, he observed the water and kept his head up to feel the fresh air that came from the sea. It was beautiful and relaxing.

Alena woke up by the sound of the door lock. At first, she was surprised that someone was opening their door and coming into the apartment, but quickly she realised that Gabriel wasn't in the bed, so it should be him opening the door. "*Maybe he went to buy something for our breakfast,*" she thought to herself. For this last week, they decided to not refill their storage. They bought the food according to their needs for the day. They did that because they didn't want to throw away food that they wouldn't use. She stood up and went to the bathroom, where he was already taking a shower, that's when she realised that he had gone running and not to buy something for breakfast.

- Good morning. – Alena said to Gabriel.
- Good morning sunshine. How did you sleep?
- You woke me up. I thought someone was invading.

Gabriel laughed, before saying:

- I am sorry that I scared you. I didn't want to wake you up.
- Actually, it was good that you did. I have to meet Anna. We combined to meet today at 9. She has work from 13:00h. I have to prepare myself.

Alena had combined to meet her long friend Anna. Anna was the only friend of Alena. She was from Slovakia and they met on the first day of university. Since then, they have become best friends.

- How was the run? – Alena asked.
- It was good. A little bit emotional though.
- Why?
- It was my last run in this city. I will miss that smooth and gentle air on my face while I am running by the seaside with that beautiful view.
- Don't worry, we will find something similar in the USA.

- I hope so.
- When I heard you, I thought that you went to buy something for breakfast.
- Oh, sorry, I didn't even think about that. Do you need something for breakfast?
- No, I will have something with Anna. I am worried about you.
- Don't worry, I will have some fruit, I may mix them and make some fruit salad.
- Will that be enough?
- Yes, it will. I am not very hungry and the anxiety doesn't allow me to enjoy the food properly.
- There is a little bit of that food from last night. You can have it, don't eat just fruit.
- Alright, I will eat something else.

Gabriel finished his shower while Alena was ready to go and meet her friend. Before leaving, she looked to the windows and exclaimed:

- Wow, it's raining!
- Really? – Gabriel was very surprised. When he was running the weather wasn't very warm but there was sunshine and he didn't expect it to rain, at least not for a few hours, or until afternoon.
- You know how the weather is here. – Alena said while kissing Gabriel. Then she took an umbrella and left, before hugging him and giving him another kiss, this time longer.

After having his breakfast, Gabriel was sitting near the window, looking at what was happening on the streets. He was looking at the streets but he wasn't paying attention to what was happening, his mind was far away. He was reflecting on the new adventure and was trying to find out what was the reason for their move. He knew that the motivation was the better work with a much better salary, but he hoped that he could find something else, something more meaningful and less material, to justify their move to another continent, far from everyone they knew. As time passed by, he began to feel uncomfortable with the thoughts in his head. He couldn't find other motivation that wasn't money. Money was the only thing leading to the decision to move to the USA. He decided to concentrate his thoughts on something else, once the idea of money being the main motive of his decisions was uncomfortable. He paid attention to the streets and saw a man on the phone. The man was dressed in a dark blue suit, black shoes, and a pink tie. He had an umbrella with him but it couldn't stop drops of rain from falling over his shoes. Gabriel thought to himself - "*Why am I paying attention to the man's clothes?*" - He realised that he was looking for an escape from the disturbing thoughts. He took a deep breath and went to make a cup of tea. They had many teas in their cupboard. Tea was their favourite drink and Alena liked to have many options at home. There was Immune Support tea, Green Energy tea, Bedtime tea, Relaxing tea, orange and vanilla tea, camomile tea, Woman's tea, which was exclusively for Alena, and Man's tea, which was exclusively for Gabriel. This last one was a strong tea with flavours of ginger and hot pepper.

Curiously, there was no English breakfast tea, the most famous and most drank tea in England. They didn't like its flavour and aroma. All the teas were well organised in the cupboard. Alena had organised them in colours in a way that when one opened the cupboard would be amazed by a colourful image that helped the soul and mind to relax way before drinking the tea. Gabriel didn't know which tea to drink, he spent about 2 minutes looking at them, trying to decide which one was appropriate for that moment. While he was still deciding the water was boiling and by the moment the kettle switched itself off, as the water had reached the ebullition point, he had made his choice, Vanilla-Orange tea. He served the tea and went back to the window. He noticed that the man was still there and, unconsciously, he started to pay attention to him again. The man was still speaking on the phone and by his movements, one could tell that he was stressed. Constantly he looked to his wrist to see the time. Gabriel realised that the man was, possibly, late and was talking about work on the phone. A Taxi came and the man got in the car and went away. Gabriel started to feel disturbed by what he had seen. It wasn't an abnormal situation, a person on the street, talking on the phone and stressed or nervous about time or something else, it was a daily thing and part of the society. But this was exactly why it disturbed Gabriel. The fact that the stress was considered a normal thing. The speed of work, the need to be on time, not miss a single minute or second, the need to want everything so perfect, and above all, the fact that shouting on the streets on the phone was no longer considered a strange thing. He asked himself why was the world like that, and he could find only one answer, Money. The engine of the world, the single thing that makes individuals, groups of people, and ultimately a whole society move their bodies and brains to do something.

"*We are all moved by the money, we wake up because of it. No one wakes up to see the sunshine, and no one goes to school merely for knowledge, but because of the money that the knowledge will bring*". - Gabriel said these words in his head. Once again, he felt uncomfortable and that disturbing feeling was growing more inside him. He decided to watch a film on the computer. He didn't know what to watch but he felt that if he immersed in the fantasies of the seventh art, it would help him to escape from the thoughts that were accusing him of feeding capitalism. He logged in to one website that produces streaming content and hosts thousands of films and TV shows that one could easily access from home. Alena and Gabriel were subscribers of one of these services and whenever they wanted to watch something such as a film, or a TV Show, they used this service.

The problem of having many choices is that it makes it difficult for one to choose and that was the dilemma that Gabriel was facing. It took him more than 5 minutes just to decide what type of content to watch. Action? No, not action. Usually, action films are filled with superheroes who get shot many times and miraculously survive, without any clear explanation, while these superheroes succeed in shooting three or four villains at the same time dodging a rain of bullets. Dramas usually have incredible stories and interesting conversations, but Gabriel didn't want something too serious. Comedy! Not even think about it. For Gabriel, the current comedy writers, or producers, were the least inspired and talented people on the seventh art. Modern comedies are based on sex and nothing more. Watching a comedy these days is like embracing the downfall of Human intelligence and creativity. With these thoughts, he managed to shorten the list of types of films to watch. An adventurous, Crime, or animation film. He then decided to watch an adventurous crime film based on a real historic event. He took the computer and went to the couch. There, he lay down and placed the computer on a small table near the couch. It was a wood table with a top base made of glass. He was still watching the film when Alena came back home. She had with her a bag with some clothes that she had bought. When Alena and Anna went out together, they liked to go to charity shops to see if they could find some clothes that they would like. Sometimes they wouldn't find anything but at this time, they did. Alena had bought a dark blue summer dress and a white shirt. She was very happy with what she had found. The charity shops were very common in England and were one of the few things that Alena truly loved. One could donate old clothes to charity shops and could also buy good clothes at a very affordable price. After taking her shoes off, Alena went straight to seat next to Gabriel. He stopped the film, changed his position and sat down.

- Hey, how are you? – Alena asked him.
- Good, just watching a film.
- Which one?
- It is about crime, you know, mafia!

- Hmm, that's good. Although those films are weird.
- Why?
- Well, I start from the principle that films are meant to give hope to good people.
- What exactly do you mean? - Gabriel asked, somehow confused.
- Well, think with me. In real life, we often see bad people winning. We see people coming from hard backgrounds, who fight every day to get a better life, and, unfortunately, in many cases, they don't succeed. Bad people always get it better. So, in films, we are supposed to see good people triumph. This will give hope to these people, right? Even if this hope is illusional, it is still hope, good hope.

Gabriel thought for a few seconds before saying something. He wasn't quite sure if he understood what Alena meant.

- So, what do you mean? With the film that I am watching? – He asked.
- Well, here is the thing. These films, of crime, usually, are about criminals who at one point hate each other and decide to kill themselves. So, it's not about the good person. None of them are good. The good person is also the bad one because he intends to hurt other people. – Gabriel kept silent, while was thoughtful. Alena decided to change the subject and talk about something else.

- Well, it doesn't matter anyway. I don't think that what I am saying is important. These things are more about entertainment, right?
- I guess.

Alena kissed Gabriel and left for the kitchen. Gabriel couldn't stop thinking about what Alena had said. The thoughts that had been disturbing him the whole day came back. He realised that the connection of things that exist in the world was deeper than what he thought. The fantasy world, which was supposed to create alternative realities that would inspire people to build a better world was also poisoned by the impurities of the real world. If the real world couldn't distinguish the good from the bad, eventually the fantasy world, which was created by people living in the real world, also wouldn't be able to distinguish these two sides. The man on the street was suffocated by the stressful life that all have. His reality was similar to everyone's, including Gabriel's. The characters of the film also lived a stressful life, and the worst of all was that the world saw this as a normal thing, as this was how the world was supposed to be.

Chapter 3

Czech Republic

Their time in the Czech Republic was good and helped them to recover the energy that they would need in their new job. During that period they visited some places in the country, spent time with friends and Gabriel had the chance to meet Alena's family. It was interesting for Gabriel to be in a different environment, he learned a lot about Alena's habits and culture and it taught him more about her identity.

Gabriel was a black man, born in Maputo, Mozambique, Africa. His father was a factory man while his mother was a commercial woman. He was the second of three siblings. The oldest one was a girl and the youngest one was also a boy. His father grew up during the years of the Mozambican revolution against Portuguese colonialism and, therefore, was a moralist and defender of education and hard work. Gabriel and his siblings were raised to be curious people, with unlimited interest in knowledge and will for inner development. Because of that, Gabriel grew as an educated person with a thirst for knowledge. He was interested in everything. There was no field of art or science that he didn't find interesting, however, history was one of his favourites. He saw history as a way of communicating with people from the past and of traveling thru times and spaces where important things had happened.

His father wanted him to become a political person and contribute to the development of the country. Gabriel had grown interested in politics inside himself and followed it for some years. However, as he was learning more and more he started to believe that being a politician was the opposite of searching for knowledge. As he was getting into politics, he felt that he was being shaped into specific beliefs. His ears were rejecting voices with different opinions and other points of view. Soon, he realized that this was not who he wanted to be and it was the opposite of what his father had taught him, and he ended up leaving the political dream behind.

When he was 17 years old he moved to Portugal to study. There he studied and lived until he was 25 years old when he moved to live with Alena. When he was about to travel to the Czech Republic, some of his friends and family from Mozambique warned him of some difficulties he would find there, because of his skin colour. However, when he arrived there he found sympathy and kindness in all the people that he met. He was happy to be in the place where Alena had grown up.

Alena's family lived in the countryside of the country, in a small village located in the mountains. It was a beautiful place, with incredible views. In the winter, the snow painted the mountains white, and the view from Alena's parent's house was incredible. When he was there, one of his favourite hobbies was walking in the forest and observing the lakes.

On the day of the trip to the USA, Alena's parents drove them to the airport in the city of Prague. Her mom cried a lot when they said goodbye to each other. The first time that Alena moved to live abroad, in the UK, was hard for her mom because at that time Alena was still searching for her identity. She still had doubts about who she was or what she wanted to do, and moving to the UK was part of discovering herself. She had come back home as a grown girl who had life plans and was more self-secure. Her mom was proud of her but she had to let her go again, and this time, to a farther place. It wasn't easy, but she saw her daughter becoming a woman, a special woman who was going to conquer the world.

"Hello, how are you? I heard you are back, I would like to meet with you. Give me a call whenever possible"

The message popped into Alena's phone, She knew who it was, and she knew that she shouldn't reply. The text message left her uneasy. It was from a man from the past with whom she had a friendship relation before. He had been interested in her but they never dated. They went out together a few times when Alena was in High school. His name was Peter. After Alena left to study in the UK, Peter still kept writing to her, expressing his desire to one day be with her, however, Alena had stopped talking to him when she started dating Gabriel. She never told him about Peter, she never thought it to be important, and until that moment, she had never thought that she would need to deal with it. She knew that she had to do something about it, but she didn't know what. She thought about it for a while, but then she told herself: - "*You are overthinking it, just ignore the message, surely he knows that I have a boyfriend. He won't write again if I ignore it*"

She deleted the message and pretended that it never happened, however the following day, when Gabriel had gone for a walk with the family dogs, Fell and Luce, Peter knocked at the door, leaving Alena astonished and worried. She had nothing to hide, but she knew that the situation wasn't ideal, still, she needed to be polite with her former friend.

- Hello Alena, nice to see you. – Peter greeted her, with a smile.

He had brought flowers and a box of chocolate for her, which he handed to her. She received it, visibly uncomfortable.

- Hey, what a surprise!
- So, how are you? English lady! – Peter said while smiling.
- I am good, thank you. What about you?
- Oh, I am good, still here in this place where nothing happens. How is England?
- It is good.

- Are you here for good or just on holiday?
- Actually, I am passing by.
- What do you mean, are you going somewhere else?
- Yes, I am home for a few days, but I am on my way to the USA.
- What? America? But you just came back after 3 years? You will be here for just a few days? I was hoping to take you somewhere, maybe we could have dinner or lunch while you tell me about England.
- Thank you, but I am here with my boyfriend. We are going to the USA for work, I am excited about it.

Visibly shocked or somehow disappointed, and feeling embarrassed, Peter said:

- Oh, I didn't know you had a boyfriend.
- It's alright.
- I feel bad for the text message and for popping here unnoticed. Please understand that I...
- It is alright, really. But I have to go now, thank you for the flowers.

Peter hugged Alena before leaving, but when he was hugging her, Gabriel was arriving home, he saw them hugging, and couldn't take his eyes off both the man and the gifts Alena was holding. It was easy to tell that she had gotten them from him, however, he didn't know who that man was. A relative? If he was a relative, why was he standing by the entrance? Did he just arrive and Alena was greeting him? There were many thoughts in his head but was interrupted by Alena:

- Hey, how was the walk?
- Was good.
- This is Gabriel, my boyfriend. Gabriel, this is Peter, a former school colleague, he heard I was around and came to see me.

Gabriel looked at Peter, not knowing exactly how to react. Alena had never told him that she had a friend so close that could come home to see her and bring her flowers. How did he know that she was home? Did she text him, was she speaking with him constantly? His thoughts were, again, interrupted, but this time by Peter, who had his hand to shake Gabriel's.

- Nice to meet you.
- Nice to meet you.
- Well, I am on my way, it was nice to see you. I wish you both a nice trip.
- Thank you. – Both Alena and Gabriel replied.

Alena knew that the situation was uncomfortable and she had to give some explanation to Gabriel. While Gabriel, was taking out his shoes and jacket, Alena decided to tell him:

- He was a colleague of mine. He came to see me, it was a surprise, I guess some of my friends must have told him that I was home.
- It is alright, I figured. He brought you some gifts.
- Yes, I am sorry, I hope it doesn't bother you. I couldn't refuse.

- No, of course, not! It would've been rude. Don't worry, I know the beautiful girl I have, and I know that I have to face competition.

They both laughed and walked into the house, hugging each other. All this situation had taken their attention away from the dogs, who had run inside the house with their muddy feet. Alena's mom shouted from the living room. They realised that the dogs had climbed on the sofas, and they ran to take them and clean them. They all laughed, but they would have to clean the sofas that were marked with mud.

Chapter 4

Life in the USA

Gabriel and Alena arrived in the USA at JFK airport. It was night when they arrived and they were very tired. They had to get another plane to Orlando, where a driver would be waiting for them to drive them to Vero Beach, the city where they would live and work. It was about 00:30 when they arrived in Orlando and as soon as they got into the car to Vero Beach, they fell asleep and slept during the whole journey. They arrived at their new home about an hour later and they went straight to sleep because on the following morning, they would wake up early to go to work.

On the first day of work, they had a meeting where they met their managers, teammates, and all the workplace. In that meeting, they were explained about the company, its values, principles, and goals.

Everyone was excited, the place was beautiful. They all knew that they would learn a lot and would get a good experience working in that place and meeting new people.

The Country Club was a private holiday centre with exclusive members. It was a place with wonderful houses, golf courses, artificial lakes, restaurants, and an equestrian centre. The members, people who belong to the *American elite,* had houses there and would go there to spend holidays, celebrate an event, or simply to spend the weekend. When these people were there, they would need servers in the restaurant, housekeepers, chefs, and people to help with horses and sports activities. These would be the roles of all the new employees that had just arrived.

When they were in the meeting room to introduce themselves, someone called the attention of Gabriel, it was a girl who, when she introduced herself, said that her name was Anne Tudor. Gabriel could not stop thinking about her. It wasn't a romantic interest, it was something else, brought up by his interest in History.

The first day at work was short, the meeting lasted 2 hours. After that, they were sent home to rest and prepare themselves for the coming days that would be harder. They were staying in a complex with many apartments, one pool, one garden, and a yard with a BBQ station. Gabriel and Alena stayed in an apartment of their own, a small, but cosy one-bedroom apartment.

After arriving home, Gabriel and Alena went to the supermarket to buy things that they would need for their everyday life. They had a lot to buy, from food to cleaning materials, bedclothes, dishes, and almost everything a house needs.

- Oh, I have no patience for this. – Exclaimed Gabriel, complaining about analysing prices, and qualities, and choosing the proper product to take home.
- Well, we need to do it. Don't you want to be in a comfortable house? – Said Alena, while she was smiling at him.
- I know, I know, but you know I am not a shopping person. You could do it because you like it.
- And what would you do? Just stay home and chill, like a lazy cat?
- Cat, yes, lazy, no. I would do other stuff.
- Come on, help me with this blanket. – Said Alena while she was handling a blanket to Gabriel.

They continued shopping, telling jokes, smiling, and very excited for this new adventure of their life. They were a beautiful couple, very supportive of each other and visibly in love. They went back home and began to clean and organize the house. Alena enjoyed organising the house. Putting the house the way she liked, decorating it with plants, flowers, paintings of her own, pictures of both of them and their family. These activities gave her a lot of joy and amusement. In the night they cooked a meal together. They both liked to eat healthy. Their choices of food were organic food, fish, vegetables, chicken, gluten-free cereals, nuts, and fruits. They didn't eat red meat and lactose products and that night they were cooking salmon with potatoes in the oven.

- I love this dish, principally the way you season the salmon. – Gabriel said it while grabbing Alena from behind.

She turned around, kissed him, and replied:

- I know you do, that is why I chose it for tonight.
- Oh, really? Can I have two portions of fish?
- No way, we will not eat all our fish just in one day, and you don't be a glutton, Mister. Now let me cook.
- Alright. But then I might be hungry.
- I know how much you eat, I have lived with you for more than a year and I cook for you. You will be alright.

While Alena was finishing cooking, Gabriel played some music. He played Nat King Cole, one of their favourite musicians. They enjoyed old-school music. They would spend the whole day just listening to slow rock ballads, Nat King Cole, Sade, Tracy Chapman, or Lauryn Hill. "When I fall in love", a song from Nat King Cole, played when Gabriel stood up and went to the kitchen. He hugged Alena from behind and kissed the back of her head. She turned around, rested her hands on his shoulders, and kissed him intensely. Then she went back to cook but Gabriel stayed there, watching her.

- Are you alright?
- Yeah, I am. Why?
- Because I know you, you are very thoughtful.

Gabriel kept silent for a few seconds, then, with a serious voice, he said:

- When we were in Portsmouth, when I was going home from work, I passed by Pubs Street.

Pub Street was a street that was always full of people who went there to frequent the bohemian nightlife. It was one of the most agitated streets of the city. But It was mostly frequented by young people, while the older ones preferred to go to the Pubs of Gunwharf Quays. Sometimes, Gabriel had two buses to get from work to home. One, his favourite would drop him in front of the flat where they lived. But this one did not operate all the hours. When he finished the work at midnight, he had no other option but to get the bus that dropped him in the city centre. From there, he had to walk for about 15 minutes before getting home. That's when he passed by Pub's Street, often crowded with noisy drunk people who, despite being university students, assembled nothing that could relate them to academic parameters. However, in this society, this was the established normalization, the academic life wasn't a life of scientific research, but a life of late-night parties with intoxicating drinks and other substances that were considered illegal, nevertheless, very well distributed and easy to commercialise and consume.

- Yes, you used that route many times. – Alena, said, with the tone of voice of someone who didn't understand the relevance of what Gabriel had said.
- Well, something always bothered me, and it still does.

- What is it?
- You see, every time that I passed that street, I saw dozens of people, mostly students, just partying. Which is not bad, but always with alcohol and drugs. I always smelled cannabis when I was on that street.

Now, Alena understood what Gabriel was saying. She knew that he didn't like to use that street. Gabriel liked people, that's why he was working in the hospitality industry. But he didn't like that street. Alena turned to Gabriel, in a gesture that showed that she was giving attention to what he was saying. Gabriel continued speaking:

- The idea that many people, principally students, can consume drugs, such as cannabis, and no one does anything, neither the authorities nor civil society, makes me question everything that our government tells us.
- What do you mean?
- Think with me, why would they allow drugs to be accessible easily and in a public place where police and other people are around if the same drugs are illegal?
- Do you think that drugs are not illegal?
- Exactly. I think that it is just a way of giving it a market value. The rules of marketing show that if a certain good or product is, for a certain reason, difficult to access, that product tends to have a high value on the market.

- Yes, that's true. But those who commercialise drugs are criminals, not the government.
- But the government doesn't seem to be interested in stopping those criminals.
- We do see news every day of drug dealers being arrested. I mean, there is corruption, some of these drug dealers are involved with the police or even with the government, and that is what makes it hard to fight it.
- Yes, I understand that and I totally agree. But my question on drugs, specifically cannabis, is that everyone can consume them with no problems. The police usually know where people consume these drugs, but they don't seem interested in stopping them.
- So, you believe that the government makes it illegal just to inflate its price?
- Yes.
- Well, I don't see how that would work. See, they have to create laws against it, they have to address funds to fight it, even if it is for faking. Don't you think that it is too much work just to inflate the price of a product that has millions of consumers? Plus they still have to face the organisations who fight for the legalisation of this drug.
- No, it is deeper than that. It is about mind-controlling.
- What! What do you mean?

- Drugs, any type of them, can disrupt the human mind. The drugs make us less conscious of reality, in a hard but simple way, we can say that they make us dumb. The governments cannot simply allow it to be legal. So, they create the illusion that it is illegal, sell it at a high price, and make money, and at the same time, they keep us dumb, in order to have control of us. That's why we get crazy about sports and nonsense things of life, but we ignore the serious ones.
- Don't you think that you are overthinking? You are becoming a conspiracy theorist.
- Maybe. But if you go outside and talk with anyone about the political life of our society, no one will seem to care. That's what the government wants, to put us away from what is really important.
- Alright, the food is ready. Can you please organise the table? – They both laughed. Gabriel played the song '*Sing for You*' by Tracy Chapman and then went to organise the table.

They ate their food while telling funny stories and laughing. They were both excited about their new adventure and they dreamed of what they had just accomplished. After eating, Gabriel cleaned the dishes while Alena was arranging the bed. They both brushed their teeth and sat to watch some Earth documentary before going to sleep. The next day would be the first day of their new job and the first time that they would ever work in the same place. New adventures and strong challenges were ahead of them. Until that day their life had been full of lessons and challenges that were pushing them, bringing out the best in them, testing their love, their trust, their commitment to staying together forever, and most importantly, testing them individually, their will and dedication of staying true to themselves and to love each other.

Chapter 5

A New Friend

When they arrived at work, Gabriel was placed to take care of a section of the restaurant together with the girl who had called his attention at the presentation meeting. Alena was going to be the hostess of the restaurant, so she was sent to organize the Menus and wine list.

Gabriel wanted to talk with the new girl from the moment he heard her name. He was very curious about her and wanted to know if she could be related to someone. That someone was Queen Elizabeth I.

They worked together for the whole lunchtime and they both enjoyed working with each other. By the end of the lunch, they had to polish some cutlery and went to the kitchen to do so. Gabriel looked at her and said:

- Can I ask you something?
- Sure?
- Yesterday, at the meeting, you said you are Anne Tudor.

- Yes, I did.
- You know Anne Boleyn, wife of King Henry VIII, both parents of Queen Elizabeth I? – She was admired. She never expected someone like Gabriel to ask her something like that.
- Well, I do, why?
- Why? Well, you have the same name as her and you carry the last name of King Henry VIII.
- It is nothing. My mom likes the name, Anne. It means *grace* and my mom says that I am a grace for her and my father. The name Tudor is common, a lot of people have it. – While saying this, Anne didn't notice that Gabriel was staring directly at her. She didn't notice that he was good at reading people's expressions.

Gabriel thought that Anne was hiding something. He couldn't tell if she was lying totally or just omitting one part of the story, but he decided to find out. He wouldn't force her to tell everything. He had just met her and didn't want to scare her. So he decided to be smooth and patient.

- Well, what a coincidence. I am sure your parents gave you the name to make a play.
- A play?
- Yes. I mean, You are Anne Tudor. I think they thought it would be interesting to give you this name.
- Yes, maybe. – She laughed.

- You know, I like the story of Anne Boleyn. I think it is very interesting.
- Really?
- Yes, I mean, it is kind of repugnant what she did, but for history readers it is interesting. – Gabriel just said that to provoke Anne. He wanted to know if she knew the story.
- I don't think she was repugnant. It is also proven that she didn't sleep with her brother. If that is what you mean. – Gabriel was happy that she knew what he was talking about. To keep provoking her, he continued:
- Well, she was killed for it.
- Yes, because there was a misunderstanding.
- Or maybe there wasn't. People who worked in the house saw them.
- Well, but she didn't do it.
- How could you know it? The story says that she was killed for it.
- The story doesn't know everything.
- And you know? – This is what Gabriel wanted. To push her until she talked about everything.

In his mind, he believed that Anne was related to the Royal House of Tudor and he thought that it would be interesting if she shared with him everything about it. He was already imagining an adventure, his imaginative mind was starting to flourish.

- Look, this is a stupid conversation. Let's finish the job and go to our pause to rest.
- Alright, I agree with you. Let us finish the job, and then we continue our conversation.

They finished polishing the cutlery and organized it in the proper space. After that, Gabriel suggested that they should fold the napkins but the manager approached them and asked them to make the mise-en-place of the room.

Alena was organizing her working station, the host station when one colleague approached and said:

- Hello, how are you? – It was one woman who worked in the management department and went to meet the new employees who had just arrived.
- I am good, thank you. – Alena answered.
- Where are you from?
- I am from the Czech Republic.
- Wow, that's wonderful. What do you think about the job, do you like it?
- Yes, I do, I am enjoying it.
- What is your name?
- I am Alena, and you?
- I am Cindy. Nice to meet you Alena, welcome to our place and I hope that you enjoy it.
- Thank you very much. Nice to meet you too. – Alena kept organizing her station when she saw Gabriel coming in with the other girl. Gabriel went straight to Alena to see how she was.

- Hey, sunshine. How is the job?
- It's good.
- Nice. I am happy that you like it.
- What will you do now?
- I will do the mise-en-place. I have to set up the whole restaurant. Just me and Anne.
- When I finish I will help you.
- Thank you sunshine.

Gabriel went back to set up the tables. He had to be close to Anne because he had to show her how to do it. He decided to bring back the conversation about Queen Anne Boleyn.

- So, you still think that Anne Boleyn didn't sleep with her brother?
- It is very crazy the way you speak about that subject. And yes, I still think so.

Alena saw them speaking, and although she couldn't hear what they were saying, she didn't mind that her boyfriend was speaking with another girl. She trusted Gabriel with all her heart, she knew that he would never disrespect her but she felt a little bit jealous. So, to avoid thinking about bad things she decided to go back to her job.

- Well, let us think. She didn't have a son and she needed to give a son to the king. She got pregnant and she lost the baby. She had to get pregnant again without the king knowing. She had to do it with someone whom she could trust and would never tell anyone. What is the best option? – Gabriel asked Anne.

- What would be the best option? Do you think that incest would be the best option? Do you really believe that?
- Maybe I don't, but the story says yes.
- The story is wrong.
- Yes, I agree that the story is wrong, and do you know why?
- Why?
- Because coming from a descendant of her family, I think that you have the truth.
- What?
- How is it to be from a royal family?
- I am not.
- Look, I am alright. I am not a bad guy. I am just interested in your story. I had never been close to a royal person before.
- I am not royal.
- Alright, a relative.
- Listen, I don't feel right to talk about this.
- Please trust me, whatever it is I can help you.
- Help me? Really? You are funny.
- Yes, I can. Just think about it. Why did you come here and why did I come here? How many people were there in that room and I am the only one who recognised your name?

- Thank you. But you can't help me. You don't even know what are you talking about. This is not a game.

After they had finished their tasks they all went to change to go home. The work was organized in two shifts. One afternoon shift, for lunch, and one evening shift for dinner. If the work was busy they would do both shifts but when it was calm they would do single shifts. On that day, the work was calm so everyone had single shifts. After finishing their shifts, everyone went home. They had a company van that drove everyone to work and back home. Alena and Gabriel sat together, on the back seats of the Van. Different from Alena and Gabriel, Anne was alone and didn't know anyone. The only person who had approached her and whom she felt comfortable talking with was Gabriel. She decided to sit next to him and Alena. They welcomed her and talked together the whole journey until home. The next day, they would work together again, on the same shift.

Chapter 6

A friend is a Guardian Angel part 1

The next day at work, Alena had the same job as the restaurant host while Gabriel had to be the server with other colleagues. Anne was working as a food runner. The shift was very calm for everyone. By the end of the service, Alena had to reorganise the menus and reservations while Gabriel and Anne had to set up the room again. Anne had been thinking about what Gabriel had said and decided to talk with him:

- Hello.
- Hi, Your Highness. – Anne laughed.
- Stop calling me that.
- Why? It is your title and I suppose that is the way I should approach you.
- Why would you approach me like that?

- I don't want to lose my head. – Anne laughed again. She was surprised by the fact that she was laughing and having fun.

Anne didn't like to be close to people. She was a reserved person and wouldn't let someone be close to her in a very short time. However, she liked the fact that Gabriel was talking to her and she felt like he and Alena would be good friends.

- Well, then you better set up this whole room while I sit down and relax. Maybe I will spare your head. – Gabriel was happy to see that Anne was opening herself. He had noticed that she seemed a sad person and it bothered him. He had just met her, he didn't know why but he wanted to help her.
- Sure, I will do so, your highness.

They continued working and about five minutes later, Anne turned to Gabriel and said:

- Can I ask you something?
- Sure.
- Why do you want to be my friend?
- What do you mean?
- Why do you want to speak with me?
- Well, I like to speak with people.
- But I don't see you speaking with other people, besides your girlfriend.

- Yes, I like to speak to people but not everyone. Just the ones that I feel are good people and can make me a better person.
- Hmm, make you a better person?
- Yes.
- So, you speak with me because I will make you a better person. So, you are using me. – Anne said that while smiling, showing that she was joking with him.
- You are funny. I like that.
- Thank you, you are too.

After they had finished their work, Gabriel went to see how Alena was. She still had to organise some restaurant dinner reservations. The shift would end in one hour and Gabriel and Anne had finished their jobs. Usually, when they finish earlier they wait in the waiting room for the van. Anne went to the waiting room. Gabriel thought about helping Alena but the manager was with her and he told her that he would wait in the waiting room.

When he arrived at the room Anne was there. She was talking on her mobile phone. He didn't want to disturb her so he decided to wait outside, in the garden. He was listening to music when Anne approached and sat close to him.

- What are you listening to?
- Just some relaxing music.
- Nice. That's cool.
- And you? Who were you talking with?
- My mother.

- How is she?
- She's good.
- How is your relationship with your family?
- It's good. – Anne said it with a sad countenance and Gabriel could understand that something wasn't right.
- You can talk to me, you know?
- Thank you. – Anne took a deep breath, closed her eyes, and said?
- I was looking for a change. – Gabriel listened carefully. Anne continued to talk.
- When I came here, I was looking for a change. You could say I wasn't the happiest girl in the world. It is all strange. – Anne was holding her tears back. Gabriel looked at her and smiled, transmitting a message that he understood her, and with a calm voice he said:
- It is alright, we all have moments when we are not happy.
- I know but this is different. I don't want to be a self-centred person but, you know, I felt like it wasn't normal what was happening, and I felt that it was my fault.
- Whatever it is, just know that everything can be solved, we can get over anything and I will be happy to help you.

- Thank you. – Anne took another deep breath and looked at Gabriel. She felt relaxed and decided to tell her story to him.
- I am the only child. My parents are good people, you can say so, but I never felt their presence. When I was little, they did what parents are supposed to do. Things like birthday parties, Christmas gifts, taking me to visit new places, and giving me all they could. It sounds right and beautiful, and it is. But the problem is they were not present. I feel like they didn't protect me from the world. They didn't teach me about friendship, the importance of learning, studying, to be careful with emotional relations. I know it may sound stupid what I am saying because everyone is raised like that. For a long time, I never thought that something was missing, I felt complete and I saw my parents as the best in the world. From very little, I had access to the internet and in my early teenage years, I knew what is porn and sex things. Plus the music I grew up listening to, is the same as everyone listens. Party music, with explicit sexual language and video clips where girls showed their bodies and made sexy dances. – After saying that, she looked at Gabriel and they both laughed.
- I know what you mean. – Gabriel said that to Anne while was still laughing. He then stopped and looked at her, he could feel what was going on with her. Gabriel had lived alone for many years, he had travelled a lot and had seen a lot of young people being lost because they lacked guidance from parents

or family. He remembered when once he felt alone in a foreign country where he knew no one, but his thoughts were interrupted by Anne as she continued to tell her story.

- As I was growing, I started to go out with friends. We would go out at night to parties. That's when I started to drink alcohol and smoke. My parents wouldn't mind that I was out, they would even let me drink when I was with them, so I thought that there was nothing wrong with drinking alcohol, getting drunk, and just having fun. – They laughed again, while they were looking at each other, knowing what they were talking about. While speaking, Anne knew that Gabriel would know what is to go to parties and get drunk and have fun with no responsibilities.

As she was talking she felt more comfortable. She had never told this to anybody else. Anne had lived her life in a self-prison. She had her pain and her fights just for herself and she was suffering from that. For the first time, she started to feel the sensation of freedom. She knew that she wasn't out of the prison yet, but she felt like standing up inside her cell, looking at the sun and feeling the sunshine hit her face, that feeling was the best that she had felt in a long time and, for that moment, it was good enough. She started to feel that even if she was never cured, what she was feeling at that moment, was good, and enough to make her stand up and learn to smile again. Then she drank a little bit of water and continued to tell her story.

- You know, from where I come from it is normal. People become teenagers, start to go out and parents just make sure that they are healthy. My parents didn't talk with me about smoking, drinking, or even dating, you know, sex. I eventually met boys and started to sleep with them. I didn't have a first love, a person to whom I would lose my virginity and feel special. It just happened with someone I met at a party.

After saying this Anne started to cry. Gabriel held her hand and smiled. He said nothing, he didn't know which words would comfort her, he didn't even know if there were words to use at that moment, but he smiled at her and with silence, managed to make her feel safe and help to heal that wound. Anne cleared her tears and said:

- It just happened and there I was, no more virgin. And I was alright with that, I believed that is how it was supposed to be, it was the way and I was just living, a young girl living the most amazing years of her life, the younger years. Talking about love was like a fairy tale or something from the past. I lost interest in school, everything was boring. I just wanted to be with my friends. Friday nights and weekends were days for parties. At one of those parties I met a boy, and I fell in love with him. We started to date and it was beautiful, I had this feeling, this butterflies around my stomach. I could enjoy watching love films, I felt emotional and wanted to be with him and make him happy. I was happy, but it didn't last long, you know. After a few months, things turned around. He used drugs and when he was drunk he would be aggressive. He was jealous and controlling. I remember one night we were out. One boy who was in the same class as me came to talk to me. We were talking about one teacher and we were laughing. My boyfriend came took my hand and dragged me out of the pub. He asked me who was the boy I was talking to. I told him that the boy was my classmate. He slapped me. – Anne put her hand to her right cheek, it was the same cheek where she got slapped.

- It was the first time, the first time that he beat me. I started to yell at him. My friends came and tried to calm us. I cried a lot but I ended up going home with him. He apologised and said that he was just confused and wanted to protect me. When we got to his home I went straight to sleep, I was really upset. The next morning we talked about what had happened. He apologised again and we were good. I thought that I had made a mistake by talking to other boys, and I blamed myself. After that, I avoided talking with other boys and I even closed my Facebook and Instagram accounts. I was doing it all for love, I loved him. But every time he was drunk he would be a different person. He would beat me and insult me. He could tell me all the worst things that you can imagine. The relationship got worse and worse. I wanted him to see me as a perfect girlfriend, so I did all to make him happy. But years passed and

> nothing changed. I had no friends, my parents didn't talk much with me, so I was lonely. He would go out with friends to get drugs and drink, and when he came home, It was ugly for me. I felt lonely, very lonely. Suddenly I started to look deep into myself and I didn't like who I was. I started to think that I hadn't grown up properly, I started to drink very soon, smoke very soon, and even weed, I smoked. And my parents, uncles, and friends thought that it was a normal thing. I ask myself what kind of society does that? You understand me! I was a child, a teenager, I didn't know what I was doing and they just let me do it. They should've protected me, even if it meant putting rules on me and forbidding me to do certain things. But I had all the freedom. I didn't know who to talk to, so I decided to move and I got this opportunity. That is how and why I am here.

Anne had her face covered in tears and she had anger in her words. Anger for the world, a world that is supposed to protect the younger ones. Society gives everything to the young ones but it gives it differently. The bad things, the world shows, advertises, and makes available everywhere and anywhere. It makes the bad things a lifestyle and a lifestyle becomes an identity. Now, for the good things, the world just makes them available, but only for the ones who seek them. It doesn't advertise them and doesn't allow an identity to be built around them. This formula of organisation destroys people and plants terror in people, Anne was just one of the victims. The biggest secret for the success of this form of organisation is that there is no one to blame. The blame always falls on the victims. But the architects of this soulless culture are the parents, the schools, the religion, the government, and the media, who just let it all go with the flow, and never look to the consequences originated from it. The mental health issues that affect a big part of young people.

Chapter 7

A friend is a Guardian Angel part 2

That day, when Gabriel was home with Alena he decided to talk with her about Anne. He knew that Alena would understand Anne and would be a good friend. Gabriel believed that Alena would be a better helper for Anne because girls understand each other better. He saw himself in the position of Anne. Gabriel himself had moments in his life when he was an outsider of society. Everything that he liked was the opposite of what people of his age liked. So, when he was out with friends or colleagues from school, he would not enjoy it. The new modern and popular music, the way of dressing, the attention to reality shows, and what he hated more, the idolatry of sportsmen and musicians. Gabriel believed that a better society should be built by talking about people who helped humanity to grow morally and scientifically, people who are known by their knowledge, their creativity, and their sense of community. Physicians, Writers, Philosophers, Politicians,

Economists, Religious. He had the idea that a society where the popular figures are sportsmen and sportswomen, pop musicians, and reality show personalities, is a doomed society. However, he would sometimes not know how to help someone who had experienced a lot of pain and developed emotional and mental health issues. That is why he turned to Alena to help Anne. He told Alena everything that Anne had told him. He did so while they were cooking dinner. Alena listened carefully. She then proposed that they invite Anne to have dinner with them. She went to her apartment and found Anne watching a film. Anne was so pleased with the invitation that it didn't matter to her that she already had her dinner prepared.

- Thank you very much. I will enjoy having dinner with you guys.
- Good, are you ready to come with me now?
- Sure, let me just wear my shoes. Sorry, you caught me by surprise I have nothing to bring.
- No need, it's our invitation, just your presence will be enough.

Anne was amazed that Alena had invited her. She knew that Alena was a good person, but it was a better feeling for her to receive the invitation from Alena and not Gabriel. They arrived at the apartment and had dinner together. They talked about a lot of things but didn't mention anything about Anne's story or situation. They had a lot of fun and Anne saw herself with people who seemed to care about her. She felt friendship and it was a weird feeling for her. She had forgotten what was a true friendship. Usually, people were with her because of the places they frequented, parties, pubs, and bars. Now she was with people who asked nothing from her, just pure friendship. For moments she felt fear, she was afraid of living an illusion. What if this friendship wasn't it? The expression on her face denounced her thoughts and Alena realised that Anne wasn't feeling alright. Alena then decided to cheer up Anne by asking her a question.

- Hey Anne, Gabriel told me that you come from Royalty. – They all laughed.
- I wish. I guess things would have been different, like for example nominating Gabriel as Prime Minister.
- Sure you wouldn't regret it. – Gabriel said that while was smiling. Anne continued the conversation and said:
- Actually, my mom decided to give me the name because she likes it. I kind of like it too. The story of Queen Anne is sad and all but it is inspiring as well. So, I guess I have a good name.
- But the most important is that you have a good soul. – Alena said that while she was touching the backs of Anne, a signal of friendship and trust.
- I am not sure, sometimes I don't even know who am I, so how could I know what kind of soul I have?

Those were profound words coming from Anne. Alena looked at her and said:

- We all have our doubts about who we are now and then. Sometimes the doubt lasts for a longer period.

We may have questions about our character, and that's when the friends come in.

Anne had some feelings that she did not recognize for a while, and she was happy.

- Thank you. I feel good and better now that I can talk with someone. I don't know how, but Gabriel managed to make me talk, even when I didn't want to.
- He is like that. He makes you talk even when you don't want to, but in the end, you find out that it's the best thing. – Gabriel kept silent. Alena looked at him and smiled, a loving smile, a trusting smile, a friendship smile. After that, she turned to Anne and said:
- Do you like stars?
- I do.
- The sky is clear, we can go outside to talk while we enjoy the cosmos view.
- That's great. Thank you for the dinner guys. I don't know how to thank you, it was really good. I will make a meal for all of us as well, but I don't know if I can match this taste.

The two girls went for a walk and Gabriel stayed home. He was writing one short story. Writing was one of his favourite hobbies, as well as watching cartoons, studying foreign languages, playing football or basketball, and listening to music. He was writing a love story, but fictional where the characters were beings from other planets. Alena and Anne went for a short walk in a park near their houses. It was a beautiful place with no light pollution. There they could see the stars in the sky, shining like fireflies decorating the roof of the universe. Alena had always loved the stars, but Gabriel had made her more interested in them. With him, she learned some constellations, some interesting curiosities about the cosmos, and the wonderful unknown size of the whole universe.

- Have you ever thought how great it is that the universe is so vast, that we may never know its real size? – Alena asked Anne while she was looking at the sky.

Anne didn't know much about the stars. She enjoyed looking at them but never actually took time to stargaze and never had thought about it. She was, however, starting to see the beauty in them and the curiosity was thriving inside her soul. The way simple things like stars could bring up a joyful smile from Alena filled her with a turmoil of feelings. A little of envy due to how easily Alena could get happy, and where she was getting the happiness from. She didn't ask much, she just needed the stars to come up and shine. She also felt relief, because she believed that for the first time, she was starting to understand what was necessary to be happy, and it was very easy to have it. She also felt thankful for the fact that she had Alena with her, a true friend who, in a simple way and without even knowing, was saving Anne.

- Not until now. - Anne answered Alena with a smile.
- It is wonderful, isn't it? The size of the Universe and everything that is out there.

- What do you think? Do you believe that there are aliens? Some Martians?- They both laughed and stayed quiet for a while. Then Anne continued:
- I wish we would know.
- Me too.
- It would change everything, and I bet it would change for the better.
- Why do you think so?
- Because we are very centred on ourselves. You know the Human being is very selfish. We care about ourselves so much. What we dress, what we eat, our work, our study, our health, our wealth. If you look, you will see that people are always thinking about these things. So if some aliens came to our planet, for the first time, we would think about something that is not us.
- I had never thought about that, but I agree.

Alena had a moment of deep reflection. Anne's words had forced her to think about what was usually occupying her mind. She then continued:

- I guess that is the problem. We believe that we are the only ones and, therefore, we put the universe around us. But I do believe that they exist and one day they will come.
- I hope they come while I am still around.
- Me too.

They continued looking at the stars and talking about the wonders of the universe. This was the start of a strong bond that would help both girls during a hard season of work. When they started their friendship, they would never know that this relation would help both of them in many situations. For a while there was silence, Anne stared at the stars as if she was hypnotised. She saw the stars all over the sky and she found herself paying attention to every detail of each star. What she felt in that moment was unique and special, the kind of sentiment that allows one to find his path in life. How could she have missed this for so long? The stars were always there for her, from the very first day that she came to this world, but she never paid attention to them. How do we miss the greatest things that are given to us, for free, and available at any time? Maybe because of their everlasting availability, we don't recognise their value. We are taught to look for the hard things, the ones that are within the reach of a few. Because of this philosophy of life, we miss the most beautiful and meaningful things.

- What are you thinking about?

The question woke up Anne. She was in a trance and she had forgotten that she was with Alena. Before answering Alena, she smiled, with her eyes always looking to the sky.

- I don't think that I was thinking. I believe that I was in another dimension.

When Anne said that they bought felt like laughing, but something held them down. They knew that Anne had reached a point inside her that would make a significant impact on her life. Alena kept listening.

- I know it may sound crazy, but it is as if I was in Heaven or something. Looking to the stars I found myself. I am happy to be here.
- I am happy that you feel that way.
- I have to thank you, Alena.
- Why?
- You listened to me, you asked about me, you asked what things I like, what is inside me.
- I guess that is just what friends do.
- Yes, but I never had that before. You know I met many people and I was always surrounded by people. Friends, family, and people who I met in pubs, discos, and on summer trips. But no one ever asked me questions about myself. No one ever asked me questions that would make me feel that someone worries about me.
- I am pleased to know that I helped you. I know what happened to you. Gabriel told me, but I didn't know it was that bad. I am happy to meet you and to be your friend.
- Thank you. You know, I think that the only thing we need, to find our path, our reason to smile, is a friend who shows empathy. With you, I feel that I found it. Thank you, Alena, thank you for being my friend.

Chapter 8

Unexpected Message

It was a Wednesday and Gabriel had work from 9 to 14 while Alena would work from 16 to 21. After work, Gabriel arrived home at about 14:45. Before leaving, Alena had cooked lunch and dinner for Gabriel, but she wouldn't be back home until at least 21:45 or 22:00. Gabriel went straight to took a shower. He warmed his food and sat down to enjoy the lovely meal that his girlfriend had cooked. While he was eating his phone rang. He looked and it was a call from his father.

- Hi, dad.
- Good morning son. – In Mozambique, it was 5 hours earlier than the east coast of the USA.
- How are you?
- I am good. But you know the reason I am calling you. Son, it's time. You need to solve your situation.
- I know dad. Give me just a little more time.

- You are out of time. You should have solved this about 2 years ago. Now you have only one year left. It is time to stop running. – Gabriel was silent. He didn't know what to say. His father knew that he needed help, but the big problem was that Gabriel didn't take any action. His father continued to talk:
- You know, there is no problem with no solution in the entire world. But it can be harder if we run from it.
- Thank you, dad. I will solve this, I promise.
- Son, things changed.
- What do you mean?
- It's not just about you now. We have only one year left. The girl has been introduced to the family. It is now that you have to decide if you come home to marry her or not. She must know, her family must know. Your girlfriend Alena, has the right to know.

Gabriel felt like losing his breath. He knew what his father's words meant. It was time for him to solve something that he had been running from for years. Gabriel belonged to the Mutah people, an ethnic group from the south of Mozambique. The Mutah people had a strong culture that they never abandoned, even in a globalized world. Among many traditions, one of the most important of the Mutah was marriage.

Traditionally, the Mutah married only people from their group, to keep their soul pure and protect their people.

This tradition existed for more than 500 years and started when the Mutah had disputes with other ethnicities.

A long time before, it was normal for Mutah Men to travel north of their region to find women or for foreign men to marry Mutah women. But the increase of foreign women and men among their people started to influence their habits. With the foreigners, came foreign gods, rituals, and language. Although the foreigners were taught the consuetudes of the Mutah, they didn't forget their own and their children would grow up with mixed cultures. With new generations coming, this led to a mix of beliefs and social problems among the Mutahs. The elders, the leaders, and the priests decided that the rising problems within the people were the result of the introduction of foreign gods in the lands of the Mutahs. The original gods were losing their power to protect their people. To solve this problem the Mutah decided that no Mutah man would marry a foreign woman and marriages would be arranged by the spirits of the ancestors.

Gabriel was raised to be a true Mutah and he knew and understood the traditions of his people. When he moved to Portugal, he knew that he had to go back to Mozambique to marry a woman that the spirits would choose for him. He grew up believing that that was the best way of marrying. He saw the example of his parents, his uncles, aunts, and grandparents. They all had married following the Mutahs tradition and were happy. At some time in his life, he was excited about the woman who the spirits would choose for him. He would lie down and imagine her, picturing his wedding day. But it changed when he met Alena. From the day he met her, his tradition started to be a nightmare in his life. He had been living the past years haunted by this obligation.

About 2 years before, when he told his father that he was in love with a foreign girl, his father warned him about the path that he was choosing. He told him that he could stay with the foreign girl, but he and she had to perform the rituals of the Mutah. He had to bring her to Mozambique and follow the Mutah's tradition to present her to their spirits and ask their permission to turn Alena into a Mutah. The ritual would also break the link that spirits had made between Gabriel and a Mutah woman.

But Gabriel didn't act and things got more complicated. The spirits had chosen the woman for him. It meant that besides bringing Alena to make the rituals he also had to make another ritual to break the link with the chosen girl. So, now he had to inform Alena about his tradition and tell her that he had a chosen wife and also had to talk with the new girl to break the link, and he had one year left, otherwise he would be forced to marry the Mutah girl.

His father had tried to advise him to open up to Alena many times but Gabriel was afraid that she wouldn't understand. He thought that her family could never understand and would never allow her to travel to Africa to be part of some tribal ritual. That is why he never told her about this issue.

- Dad, I am afraid. I don't want to lose Alena. – Tears fell from Gabriel's eyes as he was speaking. His father could tell from his voice that he was in pain and crying.
- Son, remember what I just told you. There is no problem without a solution. Things are more complicated now but, it will be alright.
- How dad, how will I solve this? I don't know what to do. I... I am afraid dad. What I did,... I did to Alena. What if the spirits don't accept her...what will I do? I messed up dad, I messed up. I should have listened to you and...talked to her sooner. Now, with a third person, it is...I don't know dad, I am sorry... - Gabriel cried loudly and his father could feel his pain. He knew that Gabriel could have already solved the situation and things could've been better. He had been stubborn, but he also knew that it was time to help him and not accuse him. So he said:
- Son, calm, please. I am here for you, I will help you. – As Gabriel was calming, his father continued:
- The first thing you need to do is to decide if you love Alena. If you love her and want to be with her, then let me know, and we will do what is necessary to make sure that you both stay together. And you need to talk with her, as soon as possible.
- But dad, what if I can't be with her, what if our ancestors don't accept a foreign woman?
- Son, is Alena the woman you want for your life?
- Of course dad, I do not doubt it.

- Then let me tell you a story.
- What story?

Gabriel was so focused on the problem that there was nothing at the moment that would make him feel better. He realised how serious his problem was and how stupid he was in ignoring the situation during the past two years, hoping that it could solve itself. He was confused and in self-punishing mode when his father said:

- It is a long story but I believe that it will help you. When I was younger, I had fallen in love with a girl from my village. I loved her, nothing would compare to her and all I wanted was to stay with her. I wanted nothing else but to be with her. You know, at that time we didn't have much. Some boys of my age dreamt about coming to the big city, to find a job and build a better life. I just thought about being with her. We both used to run all over the forest, playing around the rivers and lakes, looking at the sky, and talking about everything. But when my time to marry came, the spirits had given me another woman, and I had to follow the rules.
- This other woman was mom. I know that you will say that the spirits know what they do, that this new girl is the right one for me. I know that you and mom are happy and love each other and you will tell me that in the beginning you didn't want to marry her but you ended up falling in love and having a beautiful family and life, but my story is not yours, dad.

- Son, please let me finish the story, and then you can tell me all that you feel. Is that alright?
- Alright. I just don't want to listen to you saying that I am young and one day I will be thankful for the spirits.
- Maybe if you just listen you will know what I want to tell you.
- I am sorry dad, I am just not well now.
- I know son but listen to me.
- Alright.

After Gabriel calmed down, his father continued telling the story:

- So I was totally angry and confused. I found myself in a position that frightened me. You know, different from you, people from my generation didn't challenge the elders, we didn't face them and tell them what we thought unless they asked us. So the only thing that I thought of was running away to Maputo with the girl that I loved. I went to talk with her about that but she didn't agree with the plan. At first, I didn't understand and I thought that maybe she didn't love me the same way I loved her, but the thing is that she was wiser and calmer than I was, and she told me that if we ran, maybe we would never see our families again. We would live our lives as forsaken people. I told her that I wouldn't mind it as long as I was with her but she reminded me that we would have children and it would be fair for the children to know their family, their grandparents. And our children would need the blessing from our ancestors. You see, she showed me that it wasn't just about me and her, it was about many more people, some that were not even born yet. So I went to talk to my father to tell him that I respected the decision of the spirits but I loved another woman. My father just told me that there was no problem, I just had to break the link. You see, son, when I was stressed I didn't believe that there was a solution for my problem, I was opting for the radical one. Running away and hurt many people. But the solution was easy, I just had to talk with the elders and more experienced people. Thanks to our ancestors, I had someone who helped me, that person was your mom, with her wisdom she helped us to be together even if the spirits didn't choose us in the beginning.

- What? But I thought that you and mom were forced to marry.
- Son, our spirits are not dictators. They are not bad. Our spirits lived here before us, they felt what we feel, they would never force anyone to marry, they just help us by creating a match. But if we are not happy, they are always available to listen to us and help us with our choices, and they always make sure that our paths are lightened. Your mom was the girl that I had fallen in love with. The new girl, I talked with her and we broke the link. She is married and she is happy too, with someone that she loves.

- Wow dad, why you and mom never told me that? I always believed that you married because the spirits had chosen you.
- Some stories must be told at the right moment. This is the right moment for you to know this story.
- Thank you, dad. So, you think that this will be easy?
- You just have to be calm. Just like your mom taught me to. And be polite as well.
- Thank you, dad, so when can I talk with this girl?
- Her name is Fassie, and it is a good suggestion that you treat her by her name. I will send her contact to you and you can talk with her. I am sure that she will be nice. She is from Maputo too and therefore, I believe that she is not excited about marrying an unknown person.
- I do hope that dad. I will be waiting for the contact. And dad, what a beautiful story you and mom have. It would be a good book. - His father laughed and said:
- Sure it would son, but I quite like your story. I think that your story is truly more exciting. Maybe not for you, but it would be for the readers.
- Yeah, but I don't see the beauty in my story. I am more relaxed now but I will be better when it will be over. I don't even know how to tell Alena.
- Just trust her, maybe it will be easier than you think. And it will definitely be better than hiding it all from her.

- Yes, dad, it will. But I have to think about how will I tell her. Dad thank you for everything.
- I am your dad, you don't have to thank me.
- Is mom near you?
- Yes, she is. I will pass the phone to her.

Gabriel then spoke with his mom for about 30 minutes. She told him how they managed to marry after they talked with the elders and how their life was blessed by the spirits. She calmed him and advised him that there was no problem with no solution in the world.

After talking with his parents, Gabriel felt like a huge rock was taken from his shoulders. Some people would've said that he should ignore his culture, it was outdated and primitive. He had cousins who didn't follow any of the Mutah traditions. But Gabriel loved his culture, loved his people, and believed in his ancestors. He always wanted to get the blessing from them and wanted to share all the beauty of his culture with Alena. But the fear had made him keep secrets.

Alena was curious and liked to learn about new cultures and she was always asking questions about the life and traditions in Gabriel's home country but Gabriel never told her everything. He omitted information about some practices and would sometimes say that he didn't have a lot of knowledge about them.

A few minutes after he talked with his mother, a message came in by WhatsApp. It was his father who had just sent him the number of the girl with whom he was supposed to marry. Gabriel thought deeply about everything that his father and mother had told him. He wanted to solve the problem as soon as possible but he realised that he had to be patient and understandable. He thought about telling everything to Alena but then he imagined if this new girl, Fassie, wouldn't be that comprehensive. Some girls dream about their wedding and with their prince. What if she was waiting, her whole life, for this? Usually, girls who get into this marriage are raised to think that way by their parents. What if she was excited about meeting him, how could he break the link with her without hurting her? And what if she is one of those girls who will decide to take revenge and bring hell to his relation with Alena? He heard of stories of girls who take very personally the rejection and do unthinkable things to destroy the person who rejects them. He thought about what his father had told him, he had to put himself in her position, he had to be calm and wise.

Chapter 9

Sometimes, Love can lie

The following day, Gabriel and Alena had the same schedule. They both had single shifts, working from 9 to 14. Gabriel loved to spend time with his girlfriend. She wasn't just his girlfriend but his best friend, and the girl he would marry and spend his whole life with. But that day, he just wanted to have some time alone so that he could contact Fassie. On their way home, in the Van, Alena realised that Gabriel was very quiet. Usually, Gabriel had always something to say. Alena and Gabriel had opposite personalities. Alena was quiet while Gabriel was the one who talked more. Sometimes she would be tired of listening to his stories, or his comments on politics, or other social subjects that would come to his mind. Gabriel had a very good imagination, everything that he saw or heard, would instantly generate a reflection on him and he would want to share his thoughts with her. Alena didn't pay much attention to things, she would sometimes even be surprised by the way Gabriel would comment about something that they had seen, watched, or heard. But Gabriel wasn't a gossipy person and didn't comment about other people's lives. One thing that Alena didn't like was his comments while they were watching films. Gabriel was very critical of films. He was very restricted about what types of films to watch. He even created a category of his own for the films. The inspired and uninspired films. In his mindset, the new trend of comedies, where the jokes are, most of the time, based on sexual things or showing the inner parts of individuals, were uninspired. He saw these films as a frustrating attempt by the producers and actors to be on the big screen. On the other hand, films of drama, history, or even fiction that brought up a well-built script, and principally, with no mention or demonstration of anything related to sex, were the inspired films. He also had this strong statement that the inspired films would be found in old films, and the new films were uninspired. That is why it was very hard to take him to the cinema.

So Alena knew that if Gabriel was quiet, something wasn't right. But she didn't want to talk with him on the bus, with other colleagues around them. So she just held his hand, looked at him, smiled, and then placed her head on his shoulder. They stayed in silence the whole way until home. When they arrived home, after organising themselves, taking a shower, and eating Alena decided to bring up the conversation.

- Gabriel, what is going on? – He was expecting this question. He knew that she had noticed that something was bothering him. But he couldn't tell her, not yet.
- Nothing, sunshine. Why?

- You are weird.
- I am not.
- Please, let us not have this argument. We both know that you are weird. I know you, something is not right.

Gabriel would never convince Alena that he was all right, so the best thing to do was to make it insignificant.

- That is true, you sure know me. Look, I am sorry, I shouldn't have denied that I am weird today. I just don't want you to worry. You know, it's nothing important. I am just thinking about our plans. I am worried in a good way.
- You don't seem like that. It looks like it's something serious.
- Yes, it is. It's about our life. Look, we want to get married next year, right? So, I am thinking about all of that, about proposing to you, and...
- Wait! Are you planning those things?
- Yes, after we talked I understood that I must do something. You told me that I need to propose a year before, and I have to organise it all.
- Alright, alright. Don't tell me then, I want it to be a surprise.
- Don't spoil the surprise.
- Well, then you shouldn't show that something is not right. I mean I can't see you like that and ignore it, I have to know if everything is alright with you.

- Yes, of course, I will try to relax more and do this calmly.
- But it shouldn't be a problem, it should not get you worried that much. Why do men get stressed with marriage and weddings?
- You know what they say, it's like going to prison.
- Shut up, it's not like that. It's the most beautiful thing, it's not like a prison, it is freedom.
- Freedom? How?
- What do you mean, How?
- Well, in my point of view, I will officially belong to you and I have to wear a ring and, between me and you, in our relationship, we both know who is the boss. So, I can't imagine how it will be after we get married, your supreme powers will increase.
- Don't say that, I am not your boss, I am your sunshine.
- Yeah, that too. Come here, my sunshine boss.

They hugged each other and kissed, while Gabriel was still playing with Alena, calling her his boss and telling jokes. Alena said that she had to go to the supermarket with Anne. Gabriel saw this as an opportunity to contact Fassie. He wasn't happy about hiding things from Alena but he believed that up to that moment, that is how he would do things.

They were in this cuddling moment when a knock on the door interrupted them. It was Anne who was calling Alena to go to the supermarket as they had combined. Alena took her bag, wore her shoes, and went away. It was so quick that Anne didn't even have to get inside their apartment, however, Gabriel greeted her and they had a quick chat about work.

While Alena was out with Anne, Gabriel decided to contact Fassie. He was nervous and anxious at the same time. He took his phone, opened WhatsApp, and texted her.

- Hello, good morning.

He wrote good morning because in Mozambique it was 5 hours earlier. Instantly he received an answer.

- *Hello*

He wasn't expecting to receive an answer quickly, so he was surprised and his nervousness increased.

- *My name is Gabriel, I guess you heard about me already. I am the son of Mr. Carlos. I hope that I am not bothering you.*
- *Hi, yeah, of course, I heard about you. How are you?*
- *I am fine, thank you, and you?*
- *I am good too. You are writing from America, right?*
- *Yes, I am. From Florida.*
- *That's good. How is life there?*
- *Well, it's good, but in my case is mostly work. How are things in Maputo?*
- *Maputo is fine, you know. The hot city and always busy, there is always something going on here, something to hold our attention, although most of the time is something stupid.*

- *What do you mean by something stupid?*
- *Well, you know, there is always something a musician or another celebrity is doing that everyone is talking about.*
- *Yes, I know that. I follow everything that is happening at home.*
- *I am glad that you call here your home.*
- *Well, it is.*
- *Yes, but we have this idea that people who go away don't want to come back.*
- *Well, I think that Maputo is a beautiful place. The whole of Mozambique is. Also, it's not my choice, my soul sees Mozambique as home.*
- *Your soul?*
- *Yes, my soul. Why?*
- *I think that you should correct or protect your soul.*
- *Why?*
- *Do you think that it is good for your soul? I mean, for example, did you see the last news?*
- *Are you talking about those musicians who were fighting live on TV? Or about the religious leader who threw money on the streets?*
- *Both, and it's not all. There are many more things.*

They both sent laughing emojis. Gabriel was already calm. The beginning of the conversation had been good, up to that moment.

- *But you know, it's not just in Mozambique that those things happen, we just don't like them to happen in our home, but they are everywhere and we see them every day.*
- *Really?*
- *Yes, of course. Look at here, for example. I heard about a TV hostess who ripped her dress live. Plus, do you listen to American pop music? I mean, we are entertained by wannabes.*
- *Wow, that's exactly what I think. I just ask myself how we, as a society even allow it.*
- *You see, it's not just in our home. But of course, that doesn't justify it.*
- *Yes, it's true. But I am surprised that someone else is disturbed and disappointed with our musicians today. It is hard for me to listen to new musicians and, the worst is that I find myself alone.*
- *Well, you are not alone.*

Gabriel's last message was very powerful for Fassie. He didn't know it, he couldn't imagine that a simple message, telling someone that she or he is not alone, would have an immediate impact on that person.

- *Thank you.*
- *Why?*
- *I am sorry to tell you this, but I feel alone. Not just in entertainment.*
- *What do you mean?*

- *I haven't been good lately. Things don't come out the way they were supposed to. I am trying to hold myself, to motivate me, to find a reason, but it is not easy.*
- *I don't understand. Find a reason for what?*
- *To keep going.*
- *Is everything alright Fassie?*

Gabriel started to worry that something serious was happening to Fassie, but he also imagined that maybe she would be in the same position as him. Would she be in love with someone and, suddenly find herself in a position of marrying a stranger? Would that be the case? Gabriel was praying for it so, he decided to push the conversation and make her open herself.

- *You know, most times, things don't come out the way we imagined them. That happens with everyone. Whatever it is, you can open it to me. I am sorry if it is too soon for me to say this, but I would like to help.*
- *Thank you. I don't want to disturb you with my problems. Tell me about you, how long have you been living abroad?*
- *For a long time, more than 10 years.*
- *That is a long time. Do you think about coming back?*
- *You mean, for good?*
- *Yes.*
- *I don't know, honestly, I don't even think about it. Right now, I like to be travelling around.*
- *You are the citizen of the world.*
- *Yes, I guess you can call me that.*

- *Gabriel, thank you for writing to me. You seem to be a very nice person, I am anxious to know you even more. But now I have to go. I have things to do.*
- *You are welcome. You seem to be a nice person too.*
- *Write later, ok?*
- *I will, thank you.*
- *Kisses.*

Gabriel wasn't sure how to feel. If he should feel comfortable that he and Fassie had a good conversation and she sounded like an easy person, to whom he could explain the situation, or if he should worry because he didn't know her intentions. He decided to hide the conversation so that Alena wouldn't see it. It was hard for him to do that, but he didn't want her to ask about it before he explained the situation. He felt bad for hiding something from her, but at that moment, he believed that it was the best thing to do.

Chapter 10

Depression or game?

Gabriel and Fassie kept sending text messages to each other for a few more days. Slowly, they became distant friends and, eventually, they became friends. However, they never mentioned their arranged marriage. They didn't even talk about relationships, it was like both were trying to get to know one another before getting to that subject. But he had decided that it was time to tell her that he wasn't going to marry her. He had the love of his life with him and he wanted to break the spiritual link with Fassie.

About a week after he started to text with Fasie, Gabriel had a day off. Coincidentally it was also a day off for Alena and Anne. Anne was already a close friend of theirs. Whenever she was with them she felt good and welcomed. Alena liked to paint and Anne decided to try as well. They would spend a lot of time together, with Alena showing Anne some techniques of painting. Alena used oil painting and watercolour painting. She had many paintings in their apartment and some in her parents' home. Her favourite things to paint were nature landscapes, such as mountains, rivers, and aurora borealis. She was so fascinated by the aurora borealis that she even had one painting where she portrayed herself and Gabriel hugging under one aurora borealis. This was also Gabriel's favourite painting. But on that day off, they didn't stay home to paint. They decided to travel to the city of Orlando to the Universal Studious. They wanted to spend the day there, 3 of them, having fun. They left early in the morning with a hired car. They took with them a cooler with food and water plus a lot of fruit. Gabriel was the one driving the car. It was a calm and soft journey. They played music and commented about what they were listening and Gabriel would, from time to time, complain about how some songs were lyrically poor.

They arrived at Universal and the first thing they did was to run to the first attraction. They were having a lot of fun and amusement when Gabriel received a message on his phone. He checked the phone and it was Fassie. He looked at Alena and saw that she was very excited about one attraction. He told them that he was receiving a call from Mozambique and the girls should go without him. Alena asked if everything was alright and suggested that they should wait for him but he insisted on them going because he suspected that the call would last longer.

Alena and Anne went to the attraction and Gabriel opened his phone. He was very upset with himself because he was lying to Alena, again. He then realized that this situation was forcing him to make a lot of mistakes in his relation. Lying to his girlfriend was too much, he knew that he had to sort it out. He then decided that at that moment he would talk with Fassie about breaking the link. He opened WhatsApp and the message from Fassie said.

- Hello Gabriel, I am sorry to write to you like this. But I need to talk with someone. Could you please call me?

He was worried about what would be, but at the same time, he didn't want to get too involved with Fassie. He called her via WhatsApp and she answered his call.

- Hello, Gabriel, thank you for calling me. I hope that I am not disturbing you.

Her voice was trembling and she sounded sad. He maintained calm and said:

- It is alright, what happened? Are you crying?
- I am not good. It's not been a good day and the only person that I thought about was you. I am sorry if this is not right for you.

Gabriel was exactly where he didn't want to be. He was in that moment the person who Fassie was turning to when she needed help. This situation disturbed him because it would complicate his approach to breaking the link, but he worried about her and didn't want to hurt her, so he decided to ignore the link-breaking subject and instead, paid attention to her.

- No, it is alright, you can talk. Did something happen to you?

- Today I was supposed to meet some friends. We decided to go to the beach together. They sent me a message saying that we couldn't go because they had something to do. I was good until then, but then I saw on Instagram that they went to another place with other girls. They left me behind and lied to me. I felt down and started to cry.
- It is alright. Maybe they have an explanation. You can ask them, right?
- I know why they left me.
- Why?
- I am not a good company lately.
- Why do you say that Fassie?
- Gabriel, I have depression. Every time I am with my friends, they have to cheer me up. I am like a rock in their shoes. They keep trying to make me feel better, but it's not easy. I don't blame them, they are good friends. I guess that they wanted to have a normal girl's time without me around to bring down the atmosphere.
- Fassie, I didn't know that. I am sorry. I am here, you can talk to me.
- I had a boyfriend. I was in love with him. You know. We were together for 2 years. We had so many plans. I even thought, many times, to tell my parents that I was in love and I didn't want to get to our traditional marriage. I didn't want to have an arranged husband. But I never dared to do it. So I hid the relation for all those years. I hoped that one day I would talk to

them. A few months ago, I planned to talk with my mom first. But then I found out. My boyfriend was cheating, for many months. And the girl he was cheating with, is the one that is with my friends now. That's why I started crying and had to talk with someone.

- I am sorry to hear that Fassie. I imagine how hard it must be for you.
- When I found out, I asked my boyfriend. He was very cold with me. He told me that he didn't love me, he was just waiting for the right moment to tell me. Can you imagine that? I was about to tell my parents that I had found my love, I used to talk to him every day about that and he never said anything. He cheated on me with a girl that I knew and I used to spend time with her.
- Was she your friend?
- We were not exactly friends. She was closer to one of my friends and eventually, she was with us many times. He said many ugly things to me. I am a virgin, I told him that I wasn't ready and he seemed to understand me. He was like heaven for me. But he told me that he had always seen other girls. He blamed his cheating on me. I blamed myself too. I cried for many days. After that situation, I haven't been the same. I feel bad about myself. I can't tell my parents how I feel because I don't want to break their trust in me.
- It will be alright Fassie. I understand you and I will be here, as your friend. You will get over it, And I

don't think that it is your fault. Don't think like that, you loved someone and you told him how you felt. There is nothing to feel guilty about.

- Thank you. But since then, I don't know what to do. I feel lost. My parents have always been here for me and I feel that if I had told them from the beginning it would be easier now. When you wrote to me, I started to have something to distract me. You came as a friend and you have been helping me. I know this is too strange for you, but thank you.
- Hey, it is not strange. I feel happy that you trust me enough to open yourself to me.

By that moment Gabriel had forgotten that he had to break the link with Fassie. He worried about her emotional condition and decided that he would concentrate on helping her. Gabriel realised that things wouldn't be easier for him. He had to make a decision. Talk with Fassie about breaking the link or tell Alena what was happening. But then he thought, what if Alena didn't want him to keep talking with Fassie? If he suddenly disappeared from Fassie's life, he would be like her friends, who were forsaking her. He wanted to help her overcome the depression and then he would let her go. That meant that he had to continue to hide things from Alena.

- Listen. I will be here. You can write to me and whenever I can, I will answer you.
- Thank you, Gabriel. You have been a really good friend.

- You are a good friend too. Don't change who you are because of other people. It is not easy when we are alone. I understand that seeing your friends enjoying themselves without inviting you can be hard. But you will find out that true friends are the ones that are always there for us.
- Thank you. I will do my best to keep my head up.
- Alright. I have to go now.

Gabriel was worried about Fassie, he didn't know how he would help her but, at the same time, he knew that he had the responsibility to do it. He thought about how hard it was for her to see her friends turning their backs on her.

While he was in his thoughts, Alena and Anne came and asked him if everything was alright.

- Yes, I am. How was the attraction?
- It was good. Kind of scary. – Alena answered.
- I almost died. - Anne added.
- Come on, I don't think it was that much. You are just being girls. – Gabriel said that, joking with them.
- Or you think? I want to see how you will handle the next one. – Alena pushed him softly while saying that.
- No problem. Let's go.

They continued having fun the whole day. In the end, they went home, all happy about the amazing day that they just had.

Chapter 11

The painful truth

It was Alena's day off and Gabriel was at work. He would work the whole day so Alena had planned to clean the house during the morning and rest during the afternoon. She spent the whole morning deep cleaning the house and, after finishing, she prepared lunch and dinner. Then she rested, watching some series on the computer. However, she didn't pay attention to the scenes of the series because she started to think about Gabriel. She had noticed that lately, he was spending a lot of time on the phone, and whenever she would approach he would hide what he was doing. She believed that he was preparing the proposal. Gabriel wasn't good at hiding surprises, when he was preparing something for her, she would always know. So this time, she decided that whenever he was on the phone, she would not disturb him, she would pretend that she couldn't notice his strange attitude.

In the work, Gabriel and some of his colleagues were sent home because there wasn't much work to be done so the manager decided to stay with just 2 servers and chose the ones who had worked fewer hours than the others during that week. On the way home, Gabriel was thinking about starting the conversation of breaking the link. He worried that it would worsen Fassie's state of depression. Still, he decided to text her:

- Hello Fassie, how are you?

As always he received her answer instantly. Fassie was always expecting a message from him. Talking with him was the best part of the day for her.

- Hi, I am good, what about you?
- Me too. So, I hope that you had a nice night.
- I did. It has been better lately. Now that I have someone to talk with. I don't even have nightmares anymore.
- That is good. I am happy to know that. It's good to see that you are getting better.
- That is all thanks to you, you have been a good friend Gabriel.
- Thank you but, I just do what I can.
- It wasn't easy for me. I had hard moments, but now I have something that I am expecting, you know. It's talking with you. Now I can always expect something. Before I didn't know what to expect for my days and I had no motivation.

After reading that last message that said - "*Talking with you is what I am expecting every day*",- Gabriel placed his hand on his head. He was happy to help Fassie and to see her motivated but he didn't want to be the centre of her life. He didn't want her to be attached to him. He thought about telling her about breaking the spiritual link. He decided that he would do it that week. "*I have to, before things get more complicated*" he thought.

- We all need friends. Friends help us during hard moments. It is easier to go through difficult situations when friends are near us.
- Indeed. But what about you? How was your work? You just finished for the day, right?
- The work was good but it was very calm and they sent some of us home. I was supposed to finish later but I am on my way home now.
- What will you do when you get home?
- Probably eat something.
- What will you eat?
- I am not sure, I will see when I get home. And did you have your breakfast already?
- Yes, I did. Now I have to start preparing the lunch. Today the whole family will have lunch at home. My father didn't go to work.
- That is nice.
- Yes, it is. I like it when we are all home. Well, I have to go, I will write to you when I finish.
- Alright, have a good day. See you.
- See you, how long until you get home?

- Maybe just 20 minutes.
- OK. See you then.

After about 25 minutes Gabriel arrived home. He had hidden the conversation, as he always did, to avoid Alena finding it before he decided to open up with her. He got out of the van and went to his apartment, he passed by some colleagues who were sitting in the garden and greeted them without stopping. Alena was still in her enchanted world, thinking about Gabriel, about how much she loved him. He was the perfect man for her. He was always there for her, cared about her, and was her best friend. He always showed support and helped her to become a better person and it was he who gave her the courage to dream, with no fear. She imagined that in about a year, they would marry. Her imagination flourished and she found herself in the skies, when Gabriel came into the house, almost startling her because she wasn't expecting anyone.

- Wow, you scared me, why are you home?
- There wasn't much work today, they sent some of us home, I was one of the lucky ones. – Gabriel smiled while he was speaking and Alena ran to him to hold him tight.
- Are you alright?
- Yes, I am just happy that you are home, I missed you.
- I missed you too.
- We can spend the whole afternoon laying and relaxing. I already made dinner and if you want to eat something we have some snacks.

- Please, I want.
- Alright, go change while I prepare them.

They kissed each other and Gabriel went to change his clothes, while Alena was preparing the snacks for him. It was about 16:00 but Gabriel was supposed to be home only after 22:00, so Alena was happy that she would spend the rest of the day with him and have dinner together.

While they were sitting at the table, Gabriel eating his snacks and Alena sitting in front of him, telling him about what she had done during the day, Gabriel's phone rang. It was a WhatsApp message sound. Gabriel quickly grabbed his mobile and hid it in his pocket.

The mobile was in the middle of the table and Alena could see that it was a WhatsApp message that had just come in. She was surprised by the way he acted. He was very fast on grabbing the mobile and he had a terrified expression.

Alena looked at him but he tried to pretend that nothing abnormal had happened, so she asked him:

- Can I have your phone?
- No!... I mean, you can but, not now.
- Why?
- Nothing, it is just I...- Gabriel had difficulties justifying why he couldn't show the phone to Alena.
- Gabriel, what is going on?
- It is a surprise. If I show you I will spoil it.

It wouldn't be the first time that Gabriel hid his mobile from her because he was preparing a surprise, but he had never had any expression of fear on his face. Alena noticed that and she felt that something wasn't right.

- Show me.
- No, I can't, You know if I show you you will regret it.
- Gabriel, I am not joking, show me.
- Come on Sunshine, you know how this will end. You will be mad at me because I gave up and showed it to you.
- It is alright, but I want to see it.
- No.
- Alright, then what type of surprise and why it comes on WhatsApp? Gabriel, you will show me your phone now.

He understood that he had no choice but to show the phone to her. He took it out of his pocket and showed it to her. Alena unlocked it, saw that the message was from a girl called Fassie and it said:

"I hope that you got home safe, thank you for your messages, and for being here for me. I miss you"

Alena didn't say a word, she was confused. She and Gabriel had a strong relation and a commitment to each other, they were open books and true partners. What was that message? And who was this person? She looked at him, but he couldn't face her, he had his head down and waiting for her to say something. She just placed the phone on the table and said:

- Is there something I have to know?

He felt the world turning around at the speed of light. He had no words, he had done nothing wrong but he didn't know how to show that to Alena. He held the phone in his hand and said.

- Sunshine, I am sorry.
- What is this?
- It is a situation that I am trying to solve, and it's been hard for me to hide this from you.
- What situation, what are you talking about? Just tell me!
- I didn't want to scare or worry you.
- We have been together for a good time. In my heart, we have enough trust to open up with one another and share everything. Are you cheating Gabriel?
- No, no, I have never done that and I would never do something like that, I love you.
- I don't understand, what is going on, why can't you just tell me? -Alena said that with an enraged voice and tears starting to fall from her eyes.

Gabriel looked down, cleaned the tears that were falling from his eyes, took a deep breath, and told the story to Alena. He explained his tradition and told her who Fassie was and why he had been speaking with her. Alena was silent the whole moment, she didn't interrupt him, just listened to him until he finished talking. Then she asked:

- Why you never told me about it?
- I was thinking about doing it, but I wanted the right time.
- Alright. So, tell me something, what are you doing to solve this? In all that you told me there is nothing that you had done to break that stupid link that you talk about.
- I want to do it, but now I can't do it alone, I have to do it with the girl that was chosen for me, I mean was pointed to... you know, marry me.
- And I guess you already told her about that.
- Yes, I did.
- What did she say?
- Well, she said nothing about it yet.
- Why, what do you mean she said nothing yet?
- Sunshine listen. This has been hard for me, I want to do the right thing and protect you.
- I don't understand Gabriel, you are scaring me.

Alena had tears, she was afraid of any word that would come from Gabriel, she imagined that he would tell her that he had to go to Mozambique to meet this girl. She looked down and started to cry.

- Listen sunshine. I didn't tell her yet.
- Why, another lie? Why are you hiding things and lying to me? Do you like her? Why didn't you tell her?

- Because I was advised that we both need to break the link in peace, no one between us must feel rejected or forced to.
- I read that message, she said that she misses you. You made her your friend and you have feelings for her. You don't want her to feel rejected? What is the problem, she doesn't know you and you don't know her, how can any of you feel rejected?
- It is true what you say. But I started to talk with her and I found out that she isn't in a good moment in her life. She is depressed, because of love. She was in a relationship, but it ended badly. So I decided to be friendly with her first. I have been trying to tell her but I am not sure how this will affect her.
- Gabriel, are you worried about how this will affect her? What about how this is affecting me? Do you think about me, do you worry about me?
- Of course, I do, every time. And that is why I didn't tell you. Listen I have been talking with this girl for the last few days and all I want is to make sure that she breaks the link with no hate inside her. This is important for us, for our future. In my culture, if she feels rejected by me, my spirits, our spirits will not be happy with me. I can't be selfish, I am not forced to be with her but I can't just ignore her. I need to be careful. I understand that this may sound stupid or nonsense to you, but it is my culture. I have to follow the laws and I want to respect my ancestors, you

know how I am interested in learning more about it, I talk with you about it.

Alena was someone who always tried to respect the differences among different cultures and civilizations. She believed that there was no right or wrong culture. All the cultures had their values and had to be respected by others. She didn't understand the cultures where people are forced to marry someone who they don't know, but she respected it. But now that it was happening to her, she found it hard to respect it and she felt like a victim.

- You know I respect your culture, but I can't understand your attitude of hiding it from me.
- I am sorry, as I told you, I just wanted to protect you, I am sorry, I did it wrongly, but my intention was good, I love you.
- Can I see her?

Gabriel didn't want Alena to see Fassie, but what he feared most was that she asked to see the conversations. First, because she would find out that he had hidden them, second because of the messages that he sent to her to comfort her. He didn't want the situation to get worse. So he opened Instagram to show her. He had no message between both of them on Instagram so he thought that Alena would just see the pictures, and he hoped that after that, they would decide how to solve the situation together. He passed the phone to her. Fassie was a very attractive girl. She was good-looking and took care of her appearance. On her Instagram profile, she had pictures taken in pools and beaches, therefore, in most of the pictures she was in swimwear. Alena didn't like to see those images, she just opened WhatsApp and asked to see the rest of the conversation. Gabriel froze.

- I don't have them.
- What do you mean? Are you talking with her or no?
- Yes, I am.
- Then show me.
- I...don't think that I...
- Why? did you delete it? How many more lies Gabriel?
- Alright, I am sorry. I didn't delete them I hid them, I hid the conversation.

Gabriel took the phone from Alena, opened the conversation, and gave the phone back to Alena. She read the messages, quietly. She read all the messages and didn't miss one. He just wanted her to say something, anything, but she just read the message in silence. After reading the messages she gave the phone back to him and asked.

- Gabriel, did you, during this period, feel something, anything, for her?
- No, I didn't.

Alena took a deep breath, cleaned her tears with the back of the palm of her hand and said.

- I only see one reason for this. You have grown some type of feelings for this girl. You are interested in knowing more about her. I understand. You trust your spirits and you question yourself if this is not the best for you. They are your ancestors, how can they be wrong? So you don't want to just ignore it.

- That is not true.
- Then why didn't you tell me about this when we met? Why didn't you tell everything about your life to this girl? In these messages, you didn't mention me a single time. And Gabriel, why did you hide the conversations?
- I was just trying to find the right moment.
- Gabriel, my trust is broken. I can't believe this. If you have questions about your feelings for me, then I guess you shouldn't marry me and I shouldn't be here.
- Wait, what do you mean? C'mon sunshine, it is all just a misunderstanding, can't you see it?
- No, I can't. I can't see it, Gabriel.
- Please, let me correct this.
- Gabriel, I love you, more than anything and we both had gone through incredible things to be together. We both made sacrifices, we fought for each other. But our love must be natural, I can't be with you when I see doubts in you.

They were both crying at this moment, the tears were covering their faces, and the words coming from them were accompanied by pain.

- Please, please don't think like that, I love you, you know I do.

- I know, but I also know that you need to clear your mind. You must be prepared and sure about the steps you take. I will go to stay with Anne.
- What? No, you can't do that. We came here together and we are going to stay together, no matter what, I won't let you go away.
- I am not going away, but I also need space to think. We have work and it must not be conditioned by this situation. I am going to stay with Anne. It's just next door. You wanted to solve this on your own, so now I am giving you space. We will talk when we are both calm.

Alena took some of her things, not much, just her toothbrush, soap, hair brusher, eye lenses, work uniform, and some other clothes and went away. Gabriel was in the living room, sitting and crying.

Chapter 12

Trust Issues

That night, Alena was having difficulty sleeping, she couldn't stop thinking about what had happened. It was all of a sudden. Did she know Gabriel, if he hid something like that, would there be something else? What else didn't she know? She couldn't stop thinking about these questions.

Suddenly, she received a message on her phone:

- Hey, how are you? I hope that you are having a good time in America.

The message was from Peter. She was surprised - "*why is Peter texting me?*" - She questioned herself. A message from Peter at that exact moment? How did he know that she wasn't good? She didn't know what to do, and without thinking again, she replied:

- Hello Peter, how are you?
- I am good. Just missing you here.
- Oh, thank you.

- There's something that I have been thinking about since the last time we saw each other.
- What is it?
- I hope that I didn't create any problems for you. Your boyfriend seemed surprised when he saw me giving you flowers.
- It is alright. Don't worry about it.
- Thank you. I had to talk about that. It was good to see you the other day, you were as beautiful as ever.
- Thank you. Peter it is late here, I need to rest, tomorrow I have to work. Thank you for texting me. I needed it.
- Don't mention it. Say, can I call you tomorrow? Anytime when you are free.
- Yes, sure.
- Alright, have a nice rest.

Alena knew that it wasn't a good idea to reply to Peter's message, and even worse to tell him that she was happy for receiving a message from him. Promising to call him the next day wasn't wise either, and he probably had noticed that she wasn't good and maybe he would try to take advantage of it.

She knew that she only replied because she wanted to get her thoughts away from the situation that she was facing with Gabriel. She didn't want to lose Gabriel, she didn't want to break up with him, and she was looking for a friend or family who could advise her to solve the situation the best way possible. If Gabriel was hiding something else, she wanted to know how to make him open up, if he had done anything wrong, she wanted advice on how to make him talk, so she could forgive him. She needed him to be honest, she wanted to trust him again, and because she didn't know how to do it, she thought maybe Peter was sent to be that friend who would help. She was going to call him the following day.

Anne also couldn't sleep. Just like Alena, she couldn't stop thinking about the situation. It was all of a sudden. She had mixed emotions about it, and she felt guilty. Anne had grown fond of both Alena and Gabriel and while she knew that her feelings for Alena were purely friendship, she wasn't sure about the dimensions of her feelings towards Gabriel. He was a good friend and a good person. She had pictured herself with someone like him. He had created in her the image of a best friend and a partner, he was a reflection of a man that she would want.

"Is this all part of a bigger plan? Did I come to the USA to meet him? Is this situation now a sign that Gabriel and Alena won't last?" - She thought to herself.

It was all suspiciously well-scripted. The exact moment that she decided to leave the UK and move to the USA. She didn't plan it, it was a sudden feeling of the need for a change. Among many people at work, he was the one who approached but also who showed interest and made her feel good, he had started to heal her. What if he was the love that she was looking for? She also knew that Alena wouldn't stay in America if she and Gabriel broke up. She would go back to the Czech Republic. Alena had said it before. She wasn't so excited about this work the same way Gabriel was, but she was excited about the experience as a whole. A new challenge, in a new country, working in the same environment as him, and building their dream together. All of it, together, made the excitement. If one of these things were broken, she would lose all enthusiasm, principally, if her relationship with Gabriel was the one thing breaking. She would definitely go back home at the exact moment.

The following day, Alena got up earlier, before Anne. After washing herself, she thought about going to see Gabriel, but she was still hurt and didn't know what to say to him. She went to the living room, holding her phone and thinking about texting him, but she received a message from Peter. The message said:

- Hello, it was nice to talk with you last night. I was happy when you replied to me. I may be wrong, but I felt like something wasn't good, so I texted you. When you texted back, I was sure I had done the right thing. You know, I will always be here if you need anything. I am forever your friend.

His timing was miraculously accurate. She was shocked but also happy. He appeared in a moment that she needed a friend. Alena knew that she could talk to her family, principally her mom. Her mom would always help her and Gabriel with the best interest.

A few years ago, she and Gabriel argued. Alena was invited by her friend to a birthday party. She had a group of friends, all from her childhood. It was five of them, and they had gone together to kindergarten, primary school, and high school and had also gone to dancing classes together. They had decided to spend that birthday in Prague, where they had never been together at the same time. Alena was to travel from the UK to Prague to meet them. Gabriel didn't have problems with that, but he decided to tell her that he hoped that she and her friends wouldn't go to a discotheque by themselves.

Alena didn't agree with him, and they had a big argument. Alena decided to cancel her trip, but before that, she called her mom. Her mom explained to her that Gabriel might have been right. A nightclub is not a place for girls to go alone, not even for men who are in a relationship to go alone. A nightclub is a place of sexuality, alcohol and even drugs. It attracts people with different interests, and most of them, are looking for what is called a one-night stand. It is also a place for predators, and her mom wouldn't be comfortable knowing that Alena was in a club by herself or with her girlfriends only.

After talking to her mom, Alena understood Gabriel's perspective and knew that he wasn't trying to control her, instead, he was protecting her. She talked to him, then talked to her friends, and they decided to risk out the nightclub from their to-do list. However, she was even more surprised when two of her friends had the same feelings, their partners weren't comfortable with them going to the nightclub, and they also didn't want to, but were ashamed to tell the rest of the group. All of them were relieved that they could express themselves freely without judgment. They redesigned their trip plan and made a plan that included visiting museums, going to restaurants, going to water parks, visiting tourist attractions, and spending all their time together as friends.

However, in this situation, she wasn't ready to talk to her mom, although she knew that it would be the best decision to make. She decided to call Peter, and he picked up at the very first second his phone rang.

- Hello
- Hi Peter. Thank you for your message.
- Is everything alright with you?
- Yes, it is.
- You can tell me. You know you are alone there, but you don't need to be afraid. If there's anything, you can tell me.
- Actually, I was curious.
- Yes?
- Your text message, why did you send it?
- I had this feeling that you might need a friend. I am always thinking about you, but I also want to respect you. So I never contacted you again after that day. But yesterday, I felt like I had to.
- That's interesting.
- What happened?
- It's Gabriel, my boyfriend.
- Is everything alright with you? Did he do something?
- Well, it's complicated, I don't even know or understand it.

- Alright. I see. Look, I am here for you. You can try to explain. I will do all I can to give my support.
- Thank you. I don't know what is going on. In one moment I knew all about him, and in another, I felt like I knew nothing about him. He has this cultural thing, that has to do with his ethnicity, and... - she took a deep breath - I don't know what to say and I am embarrassed to say it. - She took another deep breath - Technically he has an arranged marriage, and he never told me about it.

She could feel the tension and the shock hitting Peter, he didn't have words and didn't know how to react. Alena was embarrassed. She thought that people would judge her. For a moment, she regretted telling that to Peter, but then he said:

- I understand. These cultural things can be tough sometimes. It is nothing for you to be embarrassed about. You didn't know. I am surprised that he never told you. I am worried about what else you don't know. You know, I have heard about some stories like that. African men move to Europe and find women to marry, while they have wives back in Africa. They are not good people, they pretend to be and deceive good people like you. It is not your shame, it is his shame.

Alena felt a strange bad feeling and started feeling uncomfortable. It was good to have someone to talk to, but his words were more disturbing than helping. She interrupted him.

- It's not like that. He is not married and has no wife. He has an arranged marriage, an obligation that he can refuse. The problem is that he didn't tell me. He says that he was afraid to tell me but, eventually, that was his goal. I am just confused now because he didn't tell me. But I know that he did nothing wrong.
- Alright, I am sorry, I didn't mean to make you feel bad.

All this time, Anne, whose bedroom was close to the living room, was listening to the conversation. She didn't have the intention of eavesdropping, but she also couldn't help herself.

Lying on the bed, she tried to ignore Alena's conversation, but she couldn't help to pay attention. Was it because she cared about Alena, or was it because of her feelings towards Gabriel?

She knew that Alena and Gabriel were facing a hard situation. She felt guilty for the thoughts she had the night before, she didn't want to be in the middle of their relationship. As much as she liked Gabriel, she knew that he loved Alena and Alena loved him. If, for some reason, this was all part of a bigger plan and Gabriel was set to be her man eventually, she wouldn't want it to be over someone's pain, principally if that someone was Alena. She thought that she had to help them. She had to be a friend, just as they had been to her. She couldn't understand what they were talking about because Alena was speaking in Czech, but she could hear when Alena mentioned the boy's name, Peter, and by the calm and soft tone of Alena's voice, she imagined that he might be a close friend or even ex-boyfriend, who could be taking advantage of Alena's situation. For some reason, still not quite clear, she felt the urge to share this information with Gabriel, but with Alena staying with her, she wouldn't be able to call or meet him without Alena's Knowledge. So she decided to text him.

- Hello Gabriel, how are you?

Gabriel, who had a rough night, full of regrets and despair, replied promptly.

- Hey Anne, I am trying to stay strong, but it is not easy. How is Alena?
- Well, that is the reason I am writing. I heard her speaking on the phone. She was talking to someone, I think that it was a friend from the Czech Republic. I didn't understand what they were speaking about, they spoke in Czech, but it seemed that he was someone close to her. Maybe a friend or...ah, a relative? I am sorry, I don't want to insinuate anything, but I didn't have a good feeling about it. Maybe it is my intuition, but I feel like you should do something, you cannot lose her. She loves and needs you, but she is confused. She just needs to trust you again, and it depends on you.

Gabriel was shocked. Who was this person? Why would Alena speak to someone else? Did she have secrets as well?

- Thank you, Anne, you are a good friend. Do you know who was she talking to?

- I think his name is Peter.

Gabriel almost fell. He remembered Peter. It was the man who had given her flowers and chocolates. The day he saw the man, he had a strange feeling, now that feeling was back, but stronger and highly uncomfortable. Who was he? What had he been to Alena? That day he didn't step into the house, just waited by the door. Now all this situation was strange. Was it a test for their love? Or was it a sign from his ancestor, or God, that he and Alena, were not meant to stay together? It was as if Fassie and Peter, had appeared to show them their destiny. Gabriel was meant to be with Fassie and Alena with Peter. He didn't like his thoughts, he was sad, but more than that, he was upset. He felt betrayed by Alena and, for the first time, he was having doubts about their love. For the first time, he felt that he didn't trust her.

Chapter 13

You broke my heart

Gabriel texted Alena, asking if they could meet. He told her that he had important things to tell her. She promptly accepted. She was uncomfortable with what Peter had said, and all she wanted was to be with Gabriel. She thought about helping him solve this situation and she had decided to forgive him, but she needed him to open up about everything. She went back home to meet him. She found him sitting in the living room. As she walked in, she could feel his nervousness. She didn't find it strange, she was nervous herself. In fact, in 2 years together, it was the first time that they had slept in different places.

- Hey, how are you? – She asked.
- I am good. You?

She just nodded her head, without saying a single word. Then she walked and sat down on the sofa. He was extremely nervous, but he had to tell her his feelings and thoughts.

- I need to ask you something, and I need you to be honest.
- Of course, I will be honest, I have always been.
- Alright. What is this Peter to you?

Alena was shocked. Why did he ask about Peter? What importance did it have in their problem? She was expecting him to open up about his situation in Mozambique. Expected him to apologise and she had already made up her mind that she would be there for him, for both of them.

- What do you mean?
- This Peter guy, he went to see you when we were in Czech, he gave you flowers and chocolates. Now you are speaking to him.

Alena couldn't believe her ears. Was he implying that she was holding secrets as well? At that moment she was upset and furious. She replied, raising her voice:

- I came here today to forgive you, to help you, help us, solve this situation. Now you saying that I am the one with secrets?
- I am not saying, I am asking.
- So what are you asking?
- Who is he, and what is your story?
- Before I answer, tell me something. What do you think? Do you think that I might have lied to you?
- I don't know, that is why I am asking. Why aren't you answering?

Alena raised her head and faced the roof, closed her eyes, took a deep breath, and with tears falling, she said:

- You know what! Alright, I will tell you. Peter was my colleague from high school. He was interested in me, and we went out maybe 2 times. But nothing ever happened between us. I was never interested in him. I was surprised when he passed by that day. I think he thought that I was back for good, and alone. He wanted to see if there was a chance, I guess. That is why he brought flowers, and he asked me out. I told him I was home for the holidays, and I was on my way to America, with my boyfriend. That was it. He wrote to me last night, I don't know why he had to write to me last night. He had never written before and neither had I to him. In a normal situation, I would not reply, but I was upset, and I thought that I could use a friend. He then called me this morning and I picked up. Do you want to know what he said?

Gabriel was quiet, visibly ashamed. Alena continued:

- He said that African men are liars, who leave their wives in Africa, go to Europe and marry other women. He said I could be one of those stupid women who fall for them. I thought that it was stupid what he had said, I was so upset, that I stopped talking to him and I decided that I had to be with you and forgive what you had done. You are the one with secrets, you are the one who lied, who hurt me, you didn't trust me enough to tell me about your culture. If you were going to marry me, didn't you want me to be part of your culture? Of who you are? But you didn't do it. And now, you are accusing me? Did you just forget the reason I had to sleep at Anne's?

Gabriel's feelings shifted from doubt regarding Alena's loyalty to shame on himself. His brain couldn't operate properly. He didn't recognise himself, he was in a place where he had never been before. In his mind, he was questioning himself - "What is happening to me? How could I accuse Alena? Am I trying to cover up my mistake by turning the tables around? Am I running away from my responsibilities, and the consequences of my actions?"

His body, automatically, sat on the chair nearby, his head down, his elbows on his lap and his palms covering his head. He was in a very dark place, ashamed, and most of all, with a big sense that he had lost control of everything. He wanted to apologise but didn't know if he should even try to talk. Alena looked at him, and now, with a calm tone, asked him?

- How did you know that I was talking with Peter?

Gabriel, still covering his head, ashamed and with a trembling voice, said.

- Anne told me. She thought that I should act quickly before I lose you for good.
- Well, you just did.

After saying that, Alena left the house and went straight to talk to Anne. Anne was walking out of the bathroom when Alena got into her apartment. Instantly, she noticed that the conversation had gone wrong, but before she had a chance to say anything, it was Alena who spoke:

- Anne, can I talk with you?
- Yes, sure. What is going on? I thought that you and Gabriel were talking.
- Yes, we did, and it wasn't good. I wish I hadn't gone to talk to him. In fact, I wish I didn't come here last night.
- Alena, what is going on?
- Did you tell Gabriel that I was talking with someone today? That I called someone?

It didn't need much for Anne to understand what had happened. She thought that she was helping them, but she had made it worse. She felt guilty, and even worse because of her feelings towards Gabriel and because of her thoughts the night before. In her mind, she saw herself as a bad person. She questioned her own acts - "*Did I create this on purpose? Did I know that this would happen?*"

She sat down, looked into Alena's eyes and said.

- I am sorry, Alena.

Alena was quiet, still standing, and looking at her, visibly sad. Anne continued:

I didn't mean to eavesdrop. I was awake and I heard you speaking with someone called Peter. I couldn't understand what you were talking about but I didn't want you to have doubts regarding Gabriel's loyalty. I thought that I could help. I believe that Gabriel loves you and I know that you love him. I wrote to him so he could come to you, open up and ask for your forgiveness. I thought that he should act fast before your doubts elevated. I am sorry, I know how it looks, but I promise I wasn't gossiping.

Alena raised her head to look up the roof, then took a deep breath, pulled a chair and sat close to Anne. Anne continued:

- I am sorry.
- It is ok, it wasn't your fault. I shouldn't have asked you like that. I understand your intentions and I believe you. Unfortunately, he is stupid, he didn't follow your advice. He questioned me, he questioned my loyalty.

Alena had tears down her face, Anne leaned forward to reach her, and with her fingers, she cleaned her tears. However, the tears continued to flow through Alena's face, and, with a crying voice, continued:

- I went there to forgive him, to support him. I was sure that I loved him and I was ready to understand that this was not an intentional mistake. But to know that, he was looking for an excuse to turn the table around, questioning me instead of asking for forgiveness, I,...I, at this moment, I don't think I can do it. I can't take it, this is all too much.
- He loves you, Alena, he must be suffering too.
- I don't know.

- I think you need to relax a bit and recover yourselves and when all is calm, you guys will be over this. I know it.

Alena and Anne hugged, and despite all the pain and stress, Alena was relieved that Anne was trying to help them, and not sabotage their relationship. It would've been too much if that had been the case. Having problems with Gabriel was something unbearable at that moment, and if her friend was a bad person, it would've made it worse. On her way to Anne's apartment, after arguing with Gabriel, Alena was thinking that after speaking to Anne, she was going to leave the job, she would prepare to go back home, to her mom. She couldn't stay in a place where she had no one. Where friends turn their backs. Her mother had told her, many times – *"Never lose your soul in the world. When things get bad, and you feel alone, remember that you have family, and we will always be here for you"* - She had never felt abandoned before. Maybe when she moved to the UK, during the first months she felt a bit lonely. But it was just the effects of a change, the first step out of her comfort zone, and therefore, she managed to go through that normally. But during that moment after arguing with Gabriel, those 45 seconds in the corridor, between both apartments, she felt her whole world falling apart. A boyfriend who had lied to her and now accusing her, and a friend who turned out to be a backstabbing person. She had her mother's words in her mind all the time, and all she could think about was *"I need to leave this cursed place"*. That was until Anne explained to her, and now, although still in pain and sad, she was happy that she had a shoulder to lean on, and she felt that it was a real shoulder, a safe place that could help her cross the desert she felt herself immersed in.

Chapter 14

A beautiful love story

Alena moved, officially, to stay with Anne, and during the first days after she moved, Gabriel's life was a storm. He wasn't the same happy and cheerful person. He would always be far away, locked in his mind. He tried to keep the concentration on work but occasionally, he would find himself forgetting or missing something when he took an order from a guest at the restaurant. This situation could have been worse if it hadn't happened with a guest that liked him. Once he took an order from a party of four guests. He missed two orders and the guests were upset. Luckily for him, one of the guests knew and liked him. He calmed everyone and helped Gabriel to correct the order.

Gabriel knew that he had to organise his life. He had to clear his mind and principally, have Alena back with him. Alena kept going to their apartment to bring him food, clean his clothes and prepare his uniform. Every day, she went to see how he was, she didn't want him to lose control of the work. She wanted Gabriel to focus and know that she loved him. She also wanted him to know that despite what happened, he could still count on her. She also needed him to realise that he had to trust her, with no secrets or doubts. She also didn't want to live with doubts in her mind and heart. She wanted to make sure that he loved her more than anything and that he would never doubt her love for him. Alena believed that leaving him alone for a few days, or weeks, would help both of them.

About 4 days after Alena moved to stay with Anne, Gabriel had a day off and decided to walk in the park close to their apartments. It was a beautiful place that he liked and used to go there whenever he wanted to relax his mind. It was about 15 o'clock and the weather was warm. The sky was blue and the trees were moving slowly on the rhythm of the smooth breeze. He was walking, lost in his thoughts when he saw Anne. She was alone, sitting on a bench and with her, she had some papers. It looked like she was writing something or drawing. Gabriel went in her direction and as he approached she noticed him. She looked at him with a smile and waved her hand. He reached her and sat on the same bench.

- Hi, Anne. How are you?
- I am fine, what about you?
- I am holding myself.
- Came for a walk to clear up your mind?
- Yes. I needed some fresh air and this place helps me. Plus the weather is so good today, I figured out that

it would help me to have a relaxed mind, at least for a few minutes.

Anne smiled. It was good to see her friend there. She knew what he was going through and she felt like she had to help him, the same way he had helped her. Since she met Gabriel and Alena, Anne had found a better version of herself. She was more motivated, she learned to dream again, and she didn't keep hard feelings and thoughts to herself anymore. She started to understand the precious gift that she had, it was herself, her life. Because of her new friends, she found hobbies. She learned to paint and draw with Alena and by reading some of Gabriel's short stories, she decided to write as well. She liked to write poems, but she started to write some short stories as well. After what Gabriel had said she smiled at him and said.

- It is good to see you here. I know how you like this place and if you are here, it means that you are finding your way.
- I am trying to, Anne.
- I know it is not easy for you Gabriel. It is not for Alena as well. But I am sure that you both will get over this and it will be alright.
- It is taking so long. It has been 4 days and she is not coming back.
- Look, she is not away. She is with me and every day she goes to see you. I see her shining when she is making your food or going to take care of your clothes. The best moments of her days are when she is doing something for you or when she is going to

see you. Alena loves you and she does not doubt it, Gabriel. It's you who must organise things. You must make a decision and show Alena that you love her and you have no doubts about your feelings. She needs to know that you never considered going to Mozambique for the other girl, even for one second. That is what is troubling her. She needs to know that you would never hesitate on your feelings for her Gabriel.

Gabriel understood at that moment how his mistake had hurt Alena. If Alena thought that Gabriel had, for once, considered the option of going to Mozambique, she must have been suffering. Feeding these thoughts on Alena was the worst part of this situation. They have been together for a good time and he had no doubts about his love for her.

- Now I see how stupid I was. I thought I was doing the right thing but I just messed up.
- It is alright. I understand you, Gabriel. I know that you love her. But this is about you and her. For Alena, your feelings for her, matter more than anyone else.
- Thank you. I do not doubt my feelings. I was caught in surprise in this situation and I respect a lot my tradition. I wanted to make sure that everyone would be alright, including the girl in Mozambique. You see, if our ancestors joined us, it is not her fault or my fault, so I can't see her as a bad person. And I don't want her or my family to see Alena as a bad

person as well. Sometimes it is so hard to do the right thing for everyone.

- You showed me something, Gabriel. You showed me that if I open my heart to people who care about me, it will be alright. You should do the same. No secrets, open your heart to Alena, your family, and this girl. Alena told me that she is in depression. You have been helping her, I am sure that she will understand you and she will be thankful for what you are doing.
- Thank you, Anne. It was good to find you here. I thank god for taking this walk today.
- It was good to find you too. It has been a while since we both sat down to talk. You know, these deep conversations that you had with me and that helped me.
- I guess we are all good friends to each other.

Gabriel smiled while saying that. He then looked at the papers that Anne had with her and asked.

- What are those papers?
- Well, hm, I am writing.
- Really?
- Yes, and you know something. I read your short story, the one where you are talking with an alien. I love that story. It inspired me and I am writing a story about a lost girl. She is found by her guardian Angel, they start to talk and the Angel eventually saves her, by showing her the most precious thing that she has.
- That sounds amazing. Is it alright if I read it?

- Not now.
- C'mon. why?
- Because I am still writing it. You will be the first to read after I have finished.
- I am curious. Please let me read it.
- Nooo. Not now, be patient.
- Alright. I am happy to see you like this. It is incredible.
- Thanks to you and Alena. You are my very best friends. I am blessed to have you.
- And we are blessed to have you too.
- You know, I should have asked this question before. How long are you guys together?
- As a couple for 2 years. But we have known each other for about 7 years.
- 7 years? Wow, how?
- It is a long story.
- Tell me.
- Now?
- Yes, tell me tell me. Oh, I love "love stories". Wow, that is funny, I said "I love, love stories". Double love.

They both laughed. Gabriel looked at Anne, she was so full of energy and positivity. He remembered the first time that he met her. She was closed, head down, and with a sad aura. She never smiled. The first look that she gave to him when he first approached her was cold. Now she was there, helping him to feel better, during the hardest moments of his life.

- Alright, I will tell you.
- Wait. I will just keep these papers in the bag. Do you want a tangerine?

Anne took two tangerines from her bag and gave one to Gabriel. She placed her two legs on the bench, crossed them, and turned to face Gabriel. She smiled at him and said.

- C'mon, start.
- Alright. Well. We met each other when I was still in university. You will not believe this but I met her online.
- What? I don't believe it.
- Yes, it is true. I remember that night like yesterday. I came back from university. I made dinner and after I ate I sat by the computer to watch a film. I lived with my cousin. He told me about this new social media site. I didn't know what was it. It was called ChatRoulette.
- I don't know it. Chat-roll-it?
- It is ChatRoulette, like a roulette.
- Alright, I see it. Interesting.
- I don't know if it still exists. That night was the only time I got there.
- Why?
- Well, let's say you would see things that would cause nightmares, or maybe make you throw up.

- What?

Gabriel laughed before continuing.

- Well, you would find all types of people there. And it wasn't beautiful.
- So, how did you find Alena there?
- Well, that is the magic of this world. Do you know when they say that God writes correctly in crooked lines?
- Yes.
- Well, that is it. I was skipping the people I would see. I just kept skipping it, like rolling the videos, you see.
- OK.
- And there I was. I saw 3 girls. They smiled and I stopped there. 2 of them greeted me and we started talking. My microphone wasn't working so I was just writing to them. They couldn't speak English, so they were using a translator to speak with me. It was so funny. We gave each other's Facebook accounts. The funny fact is that Alena said nothing the whole time. I started to talk with all of them. With time, I talked more with Alena. Every day we would send messages to each other. It was like that for 5 years.
- 5 years?
- Yes, 5 long years.
- You mean for 5 years you never met her, you didn't see her to be in the same place together?

- Yes. Just talking by messages or video call. But video calls started by the 6th year. Before that, was just messages.
- That is so romantic.
- Thank you. I was there for her. I was there to comfort her heart when it was broken. I have been there. But she was part of my life too. But in my case, I didn't tell her about my feelings, or my relationships. I was more worried about her. Our conversations were about her. When she asked about me I wouldn't be so profound.
- That was good. You cared about her.
- Yes, I did. I think that during the first year, I completely stopped talking with the two other girls. But I kept talking with Alena. I remember she used to say this very often. " *I think that you are my soulmate because I never talked with someone for that long*".

Gabriel smiled after saying that.

- That story is so beautiful. Why didn't I ask this before? It is so romantic.
- Yeah. I think that it is a beautiful story. We kept talking year after year. Then we started to watch films together.
- How did you do that?
- Well, we used to decide which film to watch. I would watch in my home and she in her home. We would start at the same time. And when we finished we would write to each other again and talk about it.

- Oh my god. It's like a book or a film. Wow. So you would sit in your home and watch a film at the same time she was doing the same in her home.
- Yes.
- She was right. You are each other's soul mates.
- She is. She is always right.
- But how did you imagine her?
- Well, I only saw her on her profile picture on Facebook and WhatsApp. I never had pictures of her. She just sent me, once a picture of her eye.
- Eye?
- Yes, don't ask me why. She just sent it to me. But I also didn't ask for pictures of her. I didn't think that it would be right. I enjoyed talking with her. I liked her personality and that was the reason I was talking to her. Her physical appearance, how she looked like, didn't matter to me.
- What about her? Did she ask for pictures of you?
- Yes, she did. She always asked me for a picture of my smile. She asked it from the first day that we talked together.
- And you gave it to her.
- No.
- Why?
- Well, I did give it to her. But only a few months before we were actually together. You know, together like physical. So, I gave it to her after 5 years.

- Why didn't you give it to her? All these years you didn't give it to her.
- I didn't think that it would be right. I couldn't send pictures to her. Her parents would worry and maybe we would be in trouble.
- That is good. You did well. It also helped you to connect spiritually. That is the best connection. Did you fall in love with her?
- Well, I liked her. But didn't get to the point of falling in love. I had girlfriends after that, and I did date girls that I had feeling for. During that period I didn't think that I would be with Alena or even meet her. There were times when I thought that we would only talk by message forever.
- That story is beautiful. Why don't you write it?
- It is not easy for me to write about my real life.
- Then maybe someone else should write.
- Yes, maybe that someone is you.
- It would be a pleasure. And then, what happened?
- We decided that we had to meet. When we started to make video calls I saw myself loving her. I questioned myself - "*How is it possible that we are still talking after so many years?*". It was just natural that we saw love in us. She went to England to study in the same year that we were talking every day. One year after that, I went to England to meet her. We met each other in London, at the Waterloo train station. I remember that when I arrived in London, I went to

the hotel where I was going to stay. She would go from Portsmouth to London, we would meet at the train station. When I was at the hotel I was nervous. I got an Uber and went to the station. I had no internet on my phone so I didn't know how to find her.

- That is beautiful and funny at the same time. So you were there just looking for her?
- Yes. I stopped at the station. I didn't know where she would be. The station is very big, and on that day, it was full of people. I think that I waited for more or less 30 minutes.
- Wow. Didn't you think that she wouldn't come?
- No, I didn't. I was sure that she was there. I waited in one place and looked to my left and there she was, coming in my direction. We hugged each other. The warmest hug I ever had until that moment.
- Wow. I am so excited about that. True love comes in so many different ways. Your story is the most incredible I have ever heard. You guys were talking for 5 years?
- 5 years.
- It is a good time to build a strong relationship. You guys will get over this situation and continue adding chapters to your lovely story.
- We have to. I will do what is right.
- As your friend, I will be here to help. Do you want to go?

- Yes, sure.

Anne and Gabriel stood up and went home. Anne was still asking questions about Gabriel and Alena. She was very excited about their story.

Chapter 15

In the hurricane's hands

It was news all over the place, everyone was talking about it. A hurricane was going to hit the city in one week. It was strange that a hurricane was going to hit Florida in the spring. Usually, the storms occur only in summer or autumn. The whole city was preparing for the arrival of the storm which had been forecasted to be the strongest one in the past 2 years. Beaches and all the facilities located in the coastal areas were closed. Gabriel, Alena, and Anne were scared and worried. None of them had ever been in a situation like that before. They had seen from the media what hurricanes were capable of and, therefore, they were worried and expecting information from their work about the situation. The company informed all the workers that there was a place where all the workers would stay during the days when the hurricane was going to pass through the city. The houses where the workers were living were not strong enough to protect them. The local government provided a sports facility building which was located in a safe area and was equipped with everything necessary to receive people. In total, there would be about 20 workers staying in the building for, at least, 2 days.

About 5 days before the hurricane hit the city, people were still doing their things normally. Although there was smooth rain and weak winds, the supermarkets, schools, roads, libraries, restaurants, and bars in the city centre were still open. The firemen and other organizations were working on strengthening the more vulnerable areas.

Gabriel was at work when the manager called everyone for an emergency meeting. It had been a strange day from the moment he had arrived at work. On that day, Gabriel was supposed to work from 9 to 22 o'clock, with a break from 13 to 17 o'clock. Usually, when they arrive at work in the morning they have to set up the esplanade, prepare the coffee, tea, water, and fold silverware. However, that day they were told not to do anything but to wait because the manager wanted to talk with them.

Everyone was anxious and some people were even nervous about the meeting. Was it about the hurricane or something else? People were asking questions to each other. One woman, who was from Mexico, raised her voice and said.

- Didn't you see it on the news?

The other workers looked at her with a surprised look.

- What was on the news? - Everyone asked.

Most of the workers were young people, with ages between 18 to 30 years old. They didn't see the news and were never updated about what was happening. Gabriel liked to see the news but not that much as well. Usually, he just opened it on the phone or computer to read the titles. If the title was about something that he considered interesting, he would open the news and read it. He didn't watch the news on the TV, in fact, he didn't watch TV at all. So, just like everyone else, Gabriel didn't know what the woman was talking about.

- The hurricane is going to arrive this night. It is coming today.

Everyone panicked and it was hard to understand what people were saying. People were complaining, asking questions, proposing solutions and some were even accusing the meteorologists of not being serious. Gabriel knew that Alena and Anne were at home, they were supposed to work in the evening. He was expecting to go home and help them prepare everything and go to the place where the company had arranged for them. He wanted to call them but preferred to wait for the management announcement first, expecting to have more information and therefore, know exactly what to tell them.

The manager came into the room and found agitation and noise. He had to raise his voice until everyone listened to him and paid attention. He explained that due to the last forecast, the work would close for the following 2 or 3 days. Everyone who was living in the workers' accommodation should move to the city centre building that had been provided by the government. They were to leave immediately, passing by their apartments to pick up only necessary items. He explained to them that the food would be provided but anyone could bring snacks if they wanted. He also told them that they shouldn't take more than 3 pieces of clothing and shouldn't worry about their electronic devices, except personal computers and mobile phones. The manager also explained that there was no time, they needed to be fast and contact anyone who wasn't at the meeting, making sure that they would be at the apartments to be picked up.

The meeting finished and the workers went all to the van to go home to pick up their things and go directly to the safe place. Four empty vans went to pick up the workers that were at the apartments. While in the van, Gabriel tried to call Alena but she didn't answer his call. He thought she didn't answer because she didn't want to talk to him. He sent messages and she didn't reply as well. He then tried to call Anne who answered the call.

- Hi, Gabriel.
- Hello Anne. How are you?
- I am fine. But do you see this rain, it's getting worse. The hurricane is announcing itself. I am kind of worried. I don't know how we will work today.
- It is worse than that.
- What do you mean?
- We are coming back home, there will be no work today. The hurricane is going to hit the city today.
- Oh my God! It was supposed to come next week.

- Yes, it got everyone by surprise. Listen, is Alena there? I am trying to call her but she doesn't answer.
- No, she is not. She went to the supermarket. She left her phone. I heard it ringing but I didn't want to answer it.
- Do you know which supermarket?
- I guess that she went to Publix, it's the nearest one and she just wanted some veggies.
- Alright. We are coming to pick you guys up. Prepare all the essential things for you and her. Hygienic things and some pieces of clothes. You can bring some snacks and your phones and computers as well. Don't bring so many things. Be ready for us. When we arrive you must be ready with your and her things, alright?
- Yes.
- Let's hope that when we arrive she will already be there.
- OK, I will do that, see you soon.
- See you.

Gabriel was worried about Alena. He was nervous during the whole journey until home. The fact that the streets were full of cars, moving slowly, increased his nervousness. Suddenly a car in front of them made a hard and string break. They looked and saw that a tree had just fallen in the middle of the street. They had to wait for the firemen to remove the tree and it took about 15 minutes until they could continue. The roads were very slippery and dangerous. Everyone was scared and feared that the hurricane would hit them while they were still on the road.

Anne did everything that Gabriel had told her to do. She prepared her and Alena's things in two bags and sat in the living room, waiting. She was hoping that Alena would come soon. She looked through the window and saw the rain getting stronger. She felt nervous because she couldn't go out and look for Alena and she couldn't call her as well. She knew that Alena had left the key of hers and Gabriel's apartment with her. She took the key and went to organize Gabriel's things as well, hoping to save time. Then she saw the vans arriving and she felt a little bit better. From the window, she saw Gabriel running. He went straight to her apartment and as soon as he arrived he asked if Alena was home already. Anne promptly answered:

- No, she didn't arrive yet.
- Alright. The rain is too strong, she probably is somewhere safe, waiting for the rain to calm.
- Yes, I also thought so. But what if it doesn't?
- Let's do this. You go to the vans. Take all that you have packed with you, and I will go after her.
- It is dangerous.
- I know, but I can't leave her alone.
- Yes, I know that, but maybe we should inform someone, like the firemen, or call the company office. They can send someone to pick her up, right?

Gabriel thought that Anne's idea was better. He called the company but no one answered the phone. The same happened with the firemen and police. He then decided to put Anne into the van while he would go after Alena. He helped Anne to take everything to the van. Everyone was already in the vans and the full ones were already leaving. When one driver saw Gabriel going back to the apartments, he called him. Gabriel stopped in the rain, already all wet and visibly worried. The driver had to raise his voice to manage to communicate with him.

- Hey! Where are you going, we have no time.
- I have to wait for someone.
- We can't wait. Other vans are coming to pick up the rest. This one can take only one more person. Let's go.
- Take someone else, I have to see If I find my girlfriend. She went to the market and didn't come back yet.
- We will call the police or the firemen and they will help. You can't go out like this. It is too dangerous.
- I know, but I tried to call them and they didn't answer.
- When we arrive there, we will be received by a team of the government, police, and firemen. We will explain them and they will help. Trust me, it is the best to do.
- I am sorry, I won't be able to go, just take someone else, I will wait for another van.

The driver didn't want to leave Gabriel there but at the same time, he knew that it would be hard to convince him to go with them. So he had an idea.

- Alright, look. When we arrive there I will let the firemen know that you are here and I will give them your number so that they contact you. Keep your phone on and always with you.
- Thank you.
- Give me your number.

Gabriel told him his number. By that time he was scared himself. He had to find Alena and make sure that she was safe. He looked at Anne who was sitting inside the van. He saw that she was afraid as well and worried about Alena. He forged a smile and shouted to her.

- It's ok. We will be fine.

Anne smiled, but she knew that Gabriel was just saying that to comfort her. She hoped that everything would be alright. The van started to move and the driver honked to Gabriel.

- Be careful. I will make sure that they call you as soon as we arrive.
- Thank you.

The van left and Gabriel went running in the direction of the supermarket. About 4 km from the apartments, there was a complex with 4 supermarkets, restaurants, and other shops. Anne had told Gabriel that Alena had probably gone to Publix, the biggest one of the 4 supermarkets. So he decided to go to Publix. He was running and the rain was hitting his face. He couldn't see more than 10 meters in front of him so he used his memory of the way to guide himself. He had used that way so many times that he knew where he would probably find stairs or other types of levels on the floor. He was exhausted but didn't stop running until he arrived at the supermarket. It was closed. He looked around to see if she would be in a covered area outside the market, but he didn't see her. He kept looking all over the complex. The complex had some palm trees and he noticed that they were waiving intensely. It seemed that they would fall and he realised that he had to be careful. The heavy rain was limiting his vision while the wind was getting strong and dangerous.

When the vans arrived at the safe place where everyone would stay, Anne went with the driver to talk with the police who were there to help them. They explained the situation and the police went straight to the Supermarket complex to look for them. A firemen's car also followed the police. Anne was guided to the room with other people. She looked and saw people talking, playing cards, board games, calling family, or watching the news on their mobile phones. She noticed how everyone was trying to relax and not let the nervousness take over them. She asked herself if she would manage to do the same. With Gabriel and Alena in danger, she couldn't relax. She held on to her phone waiting for a call. After about 30 minutes she decided to call Gabriel. He missed the call. She tried again and he answered.

- I am worried Gabriel, where are you, did you find her?

It was hard for them to hear each other. Gabriel was under a strong rain and the call was failing.

- I am ok, but I didn't find her yet. The market is closed, everything here is closed. She must be somewhere hiding from the rain and the wind. I just have to keep searching.
- Be careful.
- Alright, I will.
- The police and the firemen are going to help you. Be ready for their call.
- Thank you. I have to go Anne. Are you ok, are you safe?
- Yes, I am. Don't worry about me.
- Alright, see you.

Gabriel switched off the call and continued looking for Alena. He tried to shout out her name but he knew that his voice was drowned by the loud rain. He heard a weird noise and when he looked up it was a tree bending slowly. He moved away from it and he realised that it was falling. He feared the worst and decided to search even faster. He went to the other side of the complex, where were the restaurants. When he arrived at one restaurant that had a covered esplanade, with huge walls, he saw that something was there. As he approached he could see that it was a person. He prayed that it would be Alena. He ran and called her name out. As he was getting closer he saw that it was her. He started to cry. She hadn't seen him yet. She was on the floor, in a corner, a place where neither the rain nor the wind could reach her. She had her knees bent and her arms around them. Her head was down, between her legs. She was protecting herself. He approached slowly and touched her head. Her face was covered by tears and fear. She was scared and feeling lonely. As she raised her head, she saw Gabriel. At that moment she jumped and hugged him. The hug that she gave to him was so strong and warm that, for that moment, Gabriel didn't feel all the water from the rain that was over him, he felt warmth as if he was in the most comfortable place in the whole universe. Alena started to cry out loud and Gabriel told her that everything was fine. As he was comforting her, his phone rang. It was the police. He explained to them where he was and they went to pick them up. Two cars arrived, with their emergency lights on. One was the police and the other was the firemen. The firemen gave them warm clothes, got them into the car, and went back to the direction of the building where they would stay.

In the car, one of the firemen apologised for the delay in reaching them.

- We are sorry that it took so long to call you. The road was slippery and we had to drive slowly.
- It is alright we are happy that you guys found us. – Gabriel answered.
- We are happy that we found you, and that you are safe.

After about 45 minutes, they arrived. Anne saw them and ran to hug them. As she was hugging them, she started to cry. Alena told her to be calm because everything was alright. Some people who knew that Alena was missing approached them to give them support and show that they were happy that everyone was safe. Gabriel told Alena that Anne had brought her clothes and she could go to change.

- Anne, could you please bring her clothes?
- Sure, let me grab them.

While Anne was bringing the clothes, Gabriel looked at Alena and said.

- I was worried.
- I was too. But I knew that you would find me.
- It was a good place where you hid.
- Yes, I was still inside the supermarket when they announced that they would close because the hurricane was coming tonight. I decided to go straight home but the rain was too strong. I thought that if I waited for a little it would calm and I would be able to go home. But it didn't. I searched for a safe place to stay and that was the best I found. I was very scared Gabriel.
- I know. But you did very well.

Anne came back and gave her the clothes. Alena then said.

- What about you? Are you going to change?
- I didn't have time to pick up my things. Everything is in the apartments. I hope that my computer doesn't get the water. I don't want to lose all my work.

- Don't worry, I went there and picked up all your stuff too.

Anne said that while handing some dry clothes to Gabriel.

- Oh, thank you, Anne. Oh my God, that was very thoughtful of you.
- You are welcome.

Gabriel and Alena went to change. Alena came back before Gabriel and sat down with Anne who had prepared some snacks for them. Anne looked at Alena, gave her phone, and said:

- Never go anywhere without your phone again. You got me worried.
- I know. I left it to charge. I didn't expect to take more than 30 minutes in the market.
- It is so good to have you here safe.
- Oh, these snacks are delicious.
- Thank you. But are the same that we made together yesterday. Are you forgetting?
- No, but I didn't eat them, remember?
- Oh, that is right. We were supposed to eat them at work.

The two girls laughed and enjoyed being together in a safe place. With a more serious tone, Anne said.

- Gabriel risked his life for you. I don't think that he needs to show any other proof. You need to talk with him and help him with this situation of breaking the link.

- I know. It was incredible when he found me. I felt safe, I felt.... I don't even know how to describe it.
- A few days ago I met him in the park. We talked about both of you. He told me your story.
- He did?
- Alena, your story is the most incredible love story I ever heard. It is better than all the classic fairy tales together.
- Don't exaggerate.
- I am serious. You should have seen the look in his eyes when he was talking about you.
- What do you mean?
- He loves you. He is living the best moment of his life with you.
- Then, why did he hide and lie about that girl? He could have just told me, it was simple.
- You know men. They complicate the simple things. But he did nothing wrong. You read the messages, he never flirted or said anything to her. He was just helping her. He did choose the wrong way of doing it, but he doesn't have any feelings for anyone else. He doesn't have doubts about you.

Alena looked at Anne and then she remembered about the very first time she hugged Gabriel. The feeling was the same as the hug she gave him when he found her hiding from the rain. She turned to Anne and said.

- Thank you. I will talk with him.

Anne smiled again and passed another snack to Alena. Gabriel approached and, as he was coming, he and Alena were looking at each other straight in the eyes. He saw his life in her eyes, he saw his happiness and he imagined how impossible it would be for him to keep on if something had happened to her. In his soul, he promised himself that he would never let her go away from him, never again.

Chapter 16

Together, it is easier.

The hurricane passed. The city found itself in need of recovery. The city center didn't suffer so much damage but the whole coastal area had to be rebuilt. The roads were closed and the restaurants were being rebuilt. The hurricane had been devastating but fortunately, there were no obits. Some people had suffered injuries but no one was in difficult condition.

After 2 days, the workers of the country club went back to their apartments. They found the apartments in good condition but in need of small repairs. It took about 4 days to fix everything and during that period they didn't go to work. The restaurants were still closed and the whole country club was going through some cleaning and repair as well.

Anne decided to turn the short story that she was writing into a novel. She had written only 3 short stories and some poems, so writing a whole novel was a challenge for her, but she was enjoying and excited about what she was writing. She didn't show anyone what she was writing and when Alena asked her about it, she just told her that she had to finish it first, before showing it to anyone.

Alena was still living with Anne but was spending more time with Gabriel. They would go out together for walks and even when she wanted to go to the supermarket Gabriel was there with her. Gabriel had decided that he should talk with Fassie about breaking the link, he would tell her that he had found his love. From the day that Alena found out about Fassie, Gabriel didn't talk much with Fassie. When she sent a message he would tell her that he had so much work and that he couldn't talk at that moment. He told her that he would have 2 or 3 very busy weeks and probably during that time he wouldn't manage to call or write to her. She understood completely and asked him to write to her anytime that he could.

One day, in the afternoon he went for a walk in the park. It was a warm day with a refreshing breeze. The sky wasn't completely clear but the clouds were not enough to cover the sunshine. He was thinking about the day of the hurricane. He thought that if Alena had never left their apartment, she would never have been alone, outside, in the middle of the storm. He didn't want Alena to feel lost and lonely ever again and for that, he had to do the right thing.

He sat on a bench, held his phone in his hands, and called Fassie.

- Hello, how are you?
- I am good, and you?

- I am good too. I missed you, Gabriel. It's been a while since you said something.
- I know… I am sorry. Things have been a little complicated here.
- What happened?
- For starters, we got hit by a hurricane.
- Oh, my God. Are you alright?
- Yes, I am good. It was scary when it happened, but we are all safe.
- Thank God. I didn't hear about it and you know, I don't watch the news.
- Yes, I know. Not following the news almost brought a disaster for me. If I had watched the news I would have known and would have avoided something dangerous to happen.
- What do you mean?
- Fassie, I need to talk with you about something very serious.

Gabriel didn't know how Fassie would react but he knew what he had to do.

- Alright. I am listening.
- As you know, we have been matched by our ancestors' spirits to marry. That is why we know each other and have been talking.
- Yes, I know.
- Remember that you told me that you did have someone, who you fell in love with?

- Yes, I did fall in love with someone.
- It happened to me as well.

After saying this, Gabriel waited before saying anything else. He was expecting Fassie to say something but she kept silent. So he continued.

- I should have told you from the beginning. I am sorry for that, but I think that it is time for me to tell you more about me. I came to the USA with my girlfriend. We have been together for about 2 years. We love each other. My parents know about her and we are building our life together. When I received the information about you and I, I was scared. I didn't know what to do.

Fassie continued listening carefully, without interrupting him.

- I contacted you because I wanted to ask you to break the link but then I saw that you were not feeling good. I was afraid that if I talked with you about breaking the link while you were not good, you would get worse. I wanted to help you to feel better. I was informed that none of us should be forced to break the link and that we should be in accordance, otherwise it would bring sadness to our lives.
- Yes, that is true.

When Fassie said that, Gabriel feared that she would refuse to break the link. But he continued explaining to her.

- So, I thought that it wouldn't be good to ask you to break the link at that moment. But then, after knowing you, it wasn't anymore about the link. I wanted to help you. You became a friend to me and I worried about you. I decided to help you the way I could and not mention the link until I thought that it was safe to do.

- So, what makes you mention it now?
- I know that you have not recovered yet, but the thing is I hid all this from my girlfriend. She found out and she moved. On the day of the hurricane, she was in the city alone, she was in danger. That day, I woke up, cleaned myself, and went to work. I didn't pass by the apartment where she is staying to say hello, to see if she was ok. I almost lost her. Since then, I have decided that I need to open myself. If I have to help you, I need to do it with my heart open. You need to know my intentions as well. I made a lot of mistakes, and now I want to correct them all.

Tears fell from his eyes when he was talking about the day of the hurricane. Fassie could understand that he was crying and she said.

- Gabriel, please, don't cry.

He was surprised by her affirmation. She said it in a comforting tone that made him feel better. Fassie continued speaking.

- I am sorry that I didn't pay more attention to you. Every time that we were talking, we just talked about me. It was very selfish of me.
- No, no, it wasn't.

- I was, and I am still, happy to meet you. You became a friend in a moment of need. I believe in our ancestors and I believe that you and I are soulmates. But soulmates are not only for romantic relationships. In a moment of need, you came and gave me the energy that I needed. That was your duty as my soulmate. My friendly soulmate, the one who understood me and helped me to get over a hard moment in my life. I didn't tell you, but I feel more confident because of you. I smile more. You know, I like to sew, but for a long time, I didn't do it. I started to do it again, right now, I am wearing a shirt that I sewed myself a couple of days ago.

Fassie was also crying as she was saying this. But she was crying tears of joy. Gabriel felt happy and relieved at the same time.

- Thank you, Fassie.
- No, it's me who should be thankful. I am sorry that you had problems with your girlfriend. I will be pleased to break the link with you. I couldn't hold you. I know what I felt when my boyfriend was with another person, I could never do it with someone else.
- You can't imagine how relieved I am to hear that from you.
- Go to your girlfriend and tell her that nothing is staying between both of you.
- I will, I will tell her.

- But I have a question for you.
- What is it?
- Gabriel, you know that I follow you on Instagram, right?
- Yes, I do. I follow you too.
- Well, men are really blind sometimes.
- What do you mean?
- Well, you never thought that I could see on the pictures on Instagram that you have someone?

Gabriel was surprised that he had never thought of that. Of course, he had pictures with Alena in his profile. How had he never thought of that? He laughed at himself and said.

- Yes, you are right. We, men, are very blind.
- It is alright. Have a good day. Don't waste more time, talk with your girlfriend and bring her back to you.
- I will do it. Fassie, thank you, you are amazing.
- We are soulmates, our ancestors are never wrong.
- That is a strong truth.
- See you.
- See you.

Gabriel switched off the call and ran. He ran, with the same intensity that he had when he was running to the supermarket to find her on the day of the hurricane. But this time he wasn't going to save her from the storm, he wasn't going to save her at all. He was going to save himself.

He arrived at Anne's apartment and he knocked on the door. Anne opened the door and saw Gabriel breathing heavily. He had his arms on his knees. He was exhausted. It took a few seconds until she said something. She wasn't sure what was happening with him until he put himself straight and smiled at her. She understood his smile, it meant that Gabriel had found himself, and he was going to correct his mistakes. She smiled back at him and gave him space to get inside the apartment. She waited at the door and said:

- Don't touch that computer, My story is there and it's not ready for anyone to read. - After saying that, she went out of the apartment in a signal to clear the path for them to talk alone.

Alena was in the bedroom painting when Gabriel came to the apartment. She had headphones with her, listening to music, so she didn't realise what was happening. Gabriel approached the room, and he saw her standing, painting. She was in another world. He stayed there and admired her for a while. He knew that when Alena was painting, she would transcend to a dimension of her own. She would leave Earth and be in a place where everything obeyed only the laws that she created, and she would create those laws with her painting brush. Alena had been painting for many years. At the age of 7, her mom realised her talent and love for colours. She sent her to a painting school where she improved her techniques. Since then, she never stopped painting.

Her favourite subjects were related to the cosmos. Alena had a lot of paintings representing the stars, imaginative planets, and other celestial objects. She loved to imagine life in other worlds, with different and better behaviours. Gabriel had written some short stories inspired by her paintings and sometimes they would stay for many hours just talking about life outside their universe.

As she was painting, Alena was singing and she started to dance to the rhythm of the music that she was listening to. Because of the way that she was moving, Gabriel figured out that it would be an old-school ballad song. He then tried to guess the song. Would it be "Can't Stop Loving You" by Reo Speedwagon?, or maybe "Listen to Your Heart" by Roxette? No, probably "Weather with You" by Crowded House. Suddenly she started to sing the chorus and Gabriel was happy that he had guessed the song. Alena was listening and singing "Weather with You". She was moving so beautifully that Gabriel found himself speechless and hypnotized. While making one of her moves, Alena turned around and saw Gabriel there. She was startled but managed to hold down. She stopped, took off her headphones, and looked at him. They stayed like that for about 30 seconds. Alena then started to walk in his direction, hugged him, and kissed him.

Gabriel then looked at her and said.

- I am sorry for my mistakes. I should have never hidden things from you. Anything that happens I have to solve with you.
- Yes, we will solve everything together.

- I talked with the girl today. It's alright. She understands and she will have no problem breaking the link. It will not be a problem.

Alena was happy. She had feared that, if Fassie wouldn't accept to do it friendly, it would mess with Gabriel's head. Alena didn't worry about what would happen if Gabriel didn't break the link, but she wanted Gabriel to feel free. Knowing that Fassie would break the link friendly, was a relief for her. They kissed each other and Gabriel said.

- Will you come back home?
- I thought that you would never ask. But let's wait for Anne. We will have dinner here together and then we will go to our apartment.

Gabriel was a happy person. The happiest man in the universe. They waited for Anne. She came home, they made dinner, watched some films and enjoyed a good time as friends.

Chapter 17

You are my Soulmate

Alena and Gabriel decided that at the end of the season, which would be in about 2 months, they would travel to Mozambique, where Gabriel would break the link with Fassie. The trip would also be the opportunity for Alena to meet Gabriel's family. Alena had never been to Africa and was very excited about it. Gabriel told her many stories about it and showed her many beautiful places in videos and photos.

One day, while Gabriel was at work and Alena was home alone, she decided to read the old messages that she and Gabriel sent to each other while he was still in Portugal and she was in the Czech Republic. They had written messages to each other for 5 years until they met for the first time. As she was reading the messages, she started travelling through time.

She found herself when she was still a little girl, afraid of the world and not sure about what the future would hold for her. She remembered growing up in a small village in the

Czech Republic, and how during that time she never thought that she could leave her village to live in another place. From the moment he came into her life, Gabriel had changed her mind. It was because of him that she started to imagine life outside her comfort zone.

Her deep thoughts and reflection were interrupted by Anne who knocked at her door. Alena had forgotten that she was waiting for Anne and that they had both combined to go for a walk. Anne had to wait a few minutes until Alena was ready. They went for a walk in the same place as always, the park where they knew they would always find tranquillity and peace.

While in the park, Anne realized that Alena's mind was far away, so she asked:

- What is bothering you?
- Nothing. Why do you say that?
- I know you. First, you were not ready when I came to your apartment. You are always ready. And I can see that you are far away.
- Well, actually, it is not bothering me, it is something good.
- That is better. Is it ok to share?
- Yes, sure. And I am sorry if I am weird.
- Not a problem. I have been weird many times. – They laughed after Anne said that. Alena then said:
- You know, I think that I am reminiscing. I am going through that stage when we think about our past, we

see where we are and think about the future. All the 3 moments, at the same time. – Alena said that with a smile. Anne smiled too, she had also moments like that and, therefore, she understood Alena quite well. After looking deep into Alena's eyes, Anne said:

- I know what is it. With what I learned in the last months with you and Gabriel, I think that it is the important thing to do, to look inside us and reflect on our paths.
- Yes, exactly. You see, today when you came to the apartment, I was reading the messages that I and Gabriel sent to each other over the years. It is funny, I was a little girl and naive, but I kind of knew that something special would happen between us. Once I sent him a message when I said that we would travel the world together. When I sent that message I didn't even know Prague. I could spend a whole year without leaving my village. Now, I have been to the UK, and the USA, and will go to Africa. It is fantastic and unrealistic.

Anne saw how happy Alena was, and remembered the first time that she met Gabriel. He told her that there was a reason why he talked with her and why he was the only one who connected her name with Queen Anne Boleyn. When he said that she thought that he was crazy, but now she realised that there are things in people's lives that are written. When she decided to go to the USA, she didn't have much motivation, she didn't even know why she was going. She just wanted to get out of the confusing life that she was immersed in, in her home in the UK. Now, she had met people, friends who helped her to find herself. She looked at Alena and said:

- Some things in our lives are already written.
- Yes, I believe that now. I also believe that when we write something, we make it real. You see, I wanted to meet Gabriel, I wanted to travel with him, but I thought that it was just a wish. I thought that I would, eventually, stop talking with him and maybe one day even forget about him. Surprisingly, for 5 years, it didn't happen.
- No one can fight true love.
- That is true.
- Alena, thank you. You and Gabriel gave me something that I had been looking for for years.
- You gave it to me as well. With you, by my side, it was less painful to go through the moment when I and Gabriel were not good. I can't imagine how it would have been if you were not here.
- I guess that makes us best friends for life.
- We are already best friends for life.

Alena and Anne continued their walk and talked about their lives and next steps. With the season coming soon, Anne had decided to go to another country club in New Hampshire. It was a beautiful place, located near a big lake and a beautiful landscape. Alena and Gabriel would go to Mozambique. So, while she would wait to meet them again, she wanted to continue building herself, her personality, and self-love in a quiet and peaceful place.

Gabriel and Alena would stay more or less a month in Mozambique and then go to the Czech Republic where they wanted to see the potential of buying land where they could build their bed and breakfast project. They would stay in the Czech Republic for about 3 months until they went back to the USA again. But they still had 2 months until the end of the season and time to spend together as friends.

That night, when Gabriel was home from work he and Alena decided to go to the park to look at the stars. They had a small telescope that they had bought while were still in the UK. They took the telescope and went to a good spot in the park where they could stargaze.

That night, the sky was very clear and they could see many stars, including some planets. Gabriel loved Jupiter. He liked everything about it, the ancient mythical stories about the planet and the scientific facts about it as well. Alena's favourite thing to observe was the Orion constellation and its loyal star Sirius. They stayed almost 2 hours just looking at the sky and commenting on how beautiful the universe was.

- I hope that one day we will all be able to know more and even travel into the universe. – Gabriel said that while he was smiling. Then, Alena said:
- Maybe. But maybe we will be here no more. It will be for our children or grandchildren.
- No, I am not talking like that.

- What do you mean?
- I mean, imagine if death is just going to another universe, a gate to another dimension where we can visit many planets. How great it would be.
- It would be wonderful. There have been theories about that.
- Yes, I couldn't wait for it.
- If it exists, then I understand why no one must know.
- Why?
- Can you imagine how many people would commit suicide to go to another dimension? To look for a better life?
- That is true. It is sad, isn't it? The possibility that there are beautiful things, but they can't be revealed to us because they can be harmful.
- Yes, it is.
- Why do you think that it can be like that?
- I think that, if there is another life, that controls us, it must be very advanced that compared to it, we are like babies. So, because we are babies, some things can't be revealed to us because we can't understand them.
- Wow, that has some meaning. I hadn't thought that way before.
- But the most important is that we are thankful for this life. Do not waste it.
- Yes. Live intensely. An easy thing to do, but hard at the same time.

- I don't think that it is hard. I think that the problem is that we, Humans, created standards of success, of being important. It is like we placed an easter egg somewhere and we tell all the existing people that you will only be someone if you get that egg. And then, everyone spends their lives trying to get it. And forget what is to live.

Gabriel was surprised by what Alena had said. They talked a lot about many things, about life, but Alena would always surprise him with meaningful reflections that he would use for their lives. He stood up hugged her and kissed her, under a beautiful sky full of shining stars.

Time passed by and about a week before Gabriel and Alena traveled to Mozambique, they had combined to have lunch with Anne in their apartment. Anne arrived with an envelope. She didn't say what was it until the end of the lunch when she gave it to Gabriel.

- Thank you, what is it? – Gabriel asked.
- Remember the story that I was writing the other day? You asked to read it and I said that you had to wait.
- Yes, I do. Is this the story? But it looks more like a book, not a short story.
- Yes, I decided to make it a book. I got this beautiful inspiration and decided to make it a book, with a better story.
- That is great Anne. But tell me, are you giving me a book? I think you should publish it and then give me

a copy. – Alena, Anne and Gabriel laughed about what he had said. Anne then said:

- Well, I want to publish it. But before, I would like you to read it and tell me what you think.
- Alright, it will be my honour.
- But don't read now, read during the time you will be in Mozambique or Czech. Then tell me your opinion when we meet again here.
- Good, deal. I will enjoy reading it.

They spent the whole day together. Talking about the season that had changed their lives and had made all of them better people. Anne had learned that friendship is the biggest treasure in the world. Friends can help someone to get over anything. She was proud of opening herself to Alena and Gabriel and allowing them to save her from the demons of her past. Demons that were destroying her, silently, from inside. Before meeting them, she didn't believe that anything good would happen to her, if her parents couldn't take care of her, who else could? The world is full of quotes such as "We live in the jungle and only the strongest survive"; "Be strong and do it for yourself", and "Only you can do it", but no one was showing her how to do it or, what is it that one had to do to survive in this jungle. The more she read these quotes on social media, the less confident in herself she would be. But, with the help of friends who didn't quote anything and didn't bring any law of life, she managed to find what she needed. But most importantly, she knew that "She didn't have to do it by herself". Her friends would always be there and do it with her.

Alena was happy to complete one more journey. She had one of the hardest moments in her life when she felt that she could lose her love. She had been in the hands of a hurricane and her life was in danger. She tried to find out what she needed to improve in herself, to show Gabriel that he could trust her in anything that he needed. She wanted him to share everything that happened to him. Although she was still searching, she knew that with him, they would become a better couple, each day at a time.

Gabriel learned the importance of being true and loyal and trusting his partner in all situations. He understood that alone, he would always struggle to do whatever he wished, but with the help of people who loved him, he could always succeed. He looked at Anne's book and imagined what was it about. He thought about many things but didn't know that he was going to get one of the biggest surprises of his life, because the book that Anne had written was about him and Alena, and how they helped her. It was titled "Soulmate".